TWINS FOR THE COWBOY

TRIPLE C COWBOYS

LINDA GOODNIGHT

LJG PUBLISHING

1

Whitney Brookes leaned her forehead on the heel of her hand and wondered if she could do this.

Not that she had any choice.

Three days ago, the phone call from an Oklahoma attorney had seemed like an answer to prayer, a gift straight from God. So, she'd left the city and driven eight hours in the old dependable station wagon loaded with babies and a handful of belongings, encouraged, hopeful, and singing praise songs all the way.

She'd been on top of the world.

Until she'd gotten here.

She, Whitney Brookes, a city girl on an Oklahoma ranch, alone except for her twin toddlers and lots of very small animals she knew nothing about.

She was scared spitless.

Leaning away from the kitchen table and the piles of paperwork and indecipherable notebooks, Whitney stretched and rotated her neck. The twins were asleep, due to awaken any minute, but their long nap was time enough for her to know she was in over her head. Way over her head.

Outside a dirty kitchen window framed by yellow flowered Cape Cod curtains, her completely unexpected inheritance from a distant relative she'd barely heard of spread across forty acres in the rolling hills of Calypso County. A pretty little ranch filled with miniature animals. Tiny horses. Short, squatty cows. Sheep and goats. Fuzzy chickens.

And they were all hers. On one condition. A condition to which she'd agreed without thought or hesitation. Desperation made choices easy.

"I'm thankful, Lord. Really, I am. But I don't know anything about caring for farm animals." She'd no more than finished the sentence when a small brown horse trotted past the window.

Whitney bolted upright. The chair clattered against the butter yellow wall. She winced, hoping the twins wouldn't wake up. When no cry sounded from the back of the house, she darted out the door, crossed the porch, and spotted the miniature pony jogging merrily down the driveway and out onto the country road.

"Clive! Halt. Stop. Whoa." Or whatever she was supposed to say to a runaway horse.

As if her voice were a cracked whip, Clive broke into a dead run. Whitney gave chase. If anything happened to Clive or his friends, she was back out on the streets.

"Stop, horse. Whoa!"

Her tennis shoes slapped the dirt road, stirring enough red dust to make her blind. Did it ever rain around here?

Clive ran faster. Another pony in the pasture galloped to

the fence and whinnied as if cheering on his buddy. Clive took the encouragement to heart and galloped onward.

Racing full throttle now, her breath coming in short rasps, Whitney clenched her teeth and tasted red Oklahoma dirt. *Her* red dirt. *Hers.*

No matter how difficult the task, she would not lose this farm. Her babies needed a home, and this was it. They would not live in a shelter again. Ever.

Even if she had to wrangle animals she knew nothing about, even if she had to fall into bed exhausted every night, she would find a way to make this work.

"Stop, horsey!"

Clive's miniature hoofs battered the road like hail on a tin roof. *Clippity-clop.* The sound would have been cute if she hadn't been so desperate to catch him.

Another fifteen seconds and she'd catch up, grab that halter, shove her heels in the dirt, lean back with all one hundred twenty-five pounds and take control. But she had to catch him first.

To add insult to injury, the undersized equine kicked out behind like a bucking bronco and headed toward the side of the road, straight into a bramble of vines and thorny bushes. Even a city girl recognized the painfully sharp stickers of blackberry vines.

Sweat dripping though the day was cool, Whitney plowed into the tangle. A layer of skin peeled from her exposed legs and arms. Sweat stung the open scratches.

The horse stopped and stood still, watching her over one shoulder. Either he'd decided to be docile or he was stuck in the brambles. At only thirty-six inches high and a couple hundred pounds, Clive was small enough she could drag him home if she had to. Maybe.

She calmed her rasping breath and spoke in a soothing voice. "Come on, Clive. Be a prince. Good boy. Good boy."

Easing closer, she reached out, caught his halter. "Got you, you hairy little nuisance. Don't give me any more trouble, you hear me? The babies are asleep. We have to get back to the house before they wake up."

Even five minutes was too long to be away. With active toddlers, anything could happen in five minutes.

Worried the twins would crawl out of their crib and get hurt, she managed to edge the pony out of the weeds and onto the dirt road.

Hurry. Hurry. The babies are alone.

What kind of mother left two-and-half-year-old twins all by themselves?

But she knew the answer. The kind of mother who'd burned her bridges at age seventeen and couldn't go back. The kind who had no one to help her and no one else who even cared if her babies had food and shelter.

Home was here. With her babies. Alone. She *would* survive. And she *would* make a go of this funny little ranch. Somehow.

With a sharp tug on the halter, she convinced Clive to follow her down the road. He wasn't too happy about the detour and paused now and then to yank his head back. For a little guy, he was stout.

In a rush to get to the twins, heart still thundering from the sprint, Whitney strained forward. Clive pulled back. Her fingers slipped on the halter. She blasted him with her meanest look. His liquid brown eyes took her measure, the whites showing, nostrils blowing.

She should have brought a rope.

In the near distance, a vehicle rumbled. She picked up

her pace, worried a car would send Clive into galloping mode. She rounded the last curve, and the white farmhouse came into sight.

Some of the tension seeped from her shoulders. Almost there. The end was near.

The hum of an engine loomed closer. "Come on, boy. Good Clive."

Just when she thought the tiny horse had decided to cooperate, the very moment she grew confident and relaxed, he bolted.

Hanging tightly to the halter, Whitney kept up for a few dusty yards. Clive stretched out like a Kentucky Derby favorite, short legs flying.

Whitney jerked the halter and yelled, "Stop!" heels skidding. Clive lunged. And there on a dirt and gravel road, Whitney executed a full body face-plant.

Dirt in her mouth, her nose, her eyes, she lay still for a minute to regain her depleted air supply. Her damaged elbows and knees smarted. Road burn.

She repeated the prayer that had become her mantra, "I can do all things through Christ. I can, I can, I will."

No one had promised it would be easy, but anything was better than where she'd been. Here, at least, she had hope.

The hum of that engine grew louder. The earth rumbled. More dirt circled above her head. A door slammed.

"Ma'am, you all right?" A man dropped to his haunches next to her prone body. In her peripheral vision, Whitney spotted scuffed, round-toed western boots and faded jeans. *Lovely*. A cowboy—probably a neighbor she'd have to face for the rest of her life—had witnessed her graceless humiliation.

"Fine." She spat a mouthful of dust, flopped over and sat up.

"Let me help you." Strong hands in leather work gloves took hold of her elbows and easily lifted her to her feet.

"Thanks." The word came out gruff, embarrassed. Whitney dusted at her shirt and shorts before looking up. When she did, she lost her breath all over again.

The cowboy wasn't super tall, and no one would call him pretty, but he was a hunk, strongly built, wide at the shoulder, and as rugged as the Oklahoma frontier. A man like this could toss that ornery little horse over his shoulders and jog a mile.

With a gray Stetson pulled down over light brown hair and very attractive sun-crinkles around brown eyes, he was the kind of man dime store cowboys imitate and women ogle. Like she was doing now.

His lips moved. "Sure you're okay? Can I help you—?"

Whitney snapped into focus. Her babies. She had to get home. "Can you catch the horse?"

He spun on his boot heel and stared down the road. "That was a horse?"

Without explanation, Whitney took off in a dead run and left Mr. Rugged Cowboy in her dust.

NATE FANNED his hat against the cloud of dirt swelling around him and stared at the rapidly departing redhead. The very same redhead he'd noticed at Hammond's Feed Store yesterday. The one who'd caught his attention and lingered in his thoughts ever since.

He replaced his hat and squinted at her departing form.

He wasn't Hollywood handsome like his brothers, but he'd never scared anyone off before.

"First time for everything."

Straight, cinnamon hair flying out behind, the woman moved like an Olympic sprinter. She was about his age, maybe younger, lithe and trim without being skinny, and maybe sixteen hands high. Five-and-a-half feet in people talk. His sister, Emily, would give him a swift kick for thinking of a pretty woman in horse terms. But he was rusty in the female department. And he planned to stay that way.

Pretty. Yeah, she was, even with dirt on her face and blood running down her knees. He'd have tended to her injuries if she hadn't run off, yelling something about a horse.

"Was that really a horse?" With a shake of his head, he hopped into his truck and followed the road, figuring to catch the small critter that looked more like a dog than any horse he'd ever ridden.

"Must be one of Sally's." In his book, Sally Rogers was a little odd. Scratch that. A lot odd. A nice neighbor but not a real rancher. Not even close. But not being one to think ill of the dead, he checked himself. Sally, in her hippie skirts and wide-brimmed hats, might have been eccentric to the extreme, but she'd had a good heart and had taken good care of her livestock. Such as they were. The old woman's taste in little bitty farm animals didn't fit with his idea of raising the biggest, strongest cows and bulls possible, but she, and they, were harmless.

Anyway, Sally was gone, and, apparently, one of her animals was on the loose.

He hopped in his truck and, in moments, he passed

Sally's farmhouse and spotted the redhead darting through the front door.

"And the day gets curiouser and curiouser." He'd gone to Sally's funeral and didn't remember one single relative in attendance. Had the redhead bought Sally's farm? Was that why he'd seen her at Hammond's Feed Store yesterday?

Figuring to be neighborly if indeed she was a new neighbor, Nate drove further on and spotted a small animal with too much mane and forelock and not enough leg.

"If that's a real horse, I'll kiss it." He stopped the truck and, taking his lariat from the floorboard, got out and approached the miniature steed from the side with the soft, shushing sounds he made to all his animals, a gloved hand open as if he had a treat. He had a way with horses, with all animals, in fact.

Easy as you please, the handsome little critter plodded to him and stuck a nose into his palm. Nate grabbed the braided halter and quickly slipped the rope through the rings. "Sorry. No carrot. I cheated."

He turned the horse—for the critter *was* a horse of sorts —toward the house, aware that he'd have to leave his truck on the side of the road while he walked the stubby equine back to Sally's farm. No big deal out here in the country, and the walk wasn't far. Almost daily, he walked or rode his horse for miles on the ranch, up and down ravines, through canyons, over high hills, through creeks and woods. Walking was part of ranch life, though he was fond of his three-quarter ton truck and his favorite gelding, Uncle Buck. A real horse.

One hand on the rope, he reached, shut off the engine, and took the keys.

In five minutes, he stepped up on Sally's long covered

porch, his boots noisy on the wood, and knocked. The little stallion stepped right up with him as if accustomed to this sort of afternoon adventure. Not surprising. He'd heard Sally sometimes let her animals live in the house with her.

From inside, he heard crying. He knocked harder. Maybe the redhead was hurt worse than she let on. Maybe she'd broken that scraped and bloody arm.

He should have offered help. He should have paid more attention. He should have insisted on driving her home. Guilt flooded in. Guilt and bad memories. He never seemed to notice the important things in time to fix them.

The door whipped open. The redhead held a tear-stained toddler on one hip while an identical child clung to her bleeding kneecap with one arm and clutched a stuffed animal in the other. His gaze went from one baby to the other. Twins. They had to be.

He didn't recall seeing babies at the Feed Store. Had they been in the backseat of that old station wagon?

"Uh." Nate floundered, off balance. "I found your...uh... horse." He'd almost said dog. Except his dogs were bigger than this living, breathing stuffed animal.

"Thank you." She stepped outside, dragging the floor toddler on her leg as she reached for the rope. "I'll put him in the pen."

With those babies hanging on her like possums?

"I'll do it. Show me where."

"I don't know." An expression he could only describe as hopeless creased her face. "Anywhere that will hold him. This is the third time in two days he's escaped."

If she wanted him to stay put, she should put him some-where secure. Pretty easy decision from Nate's viewpoint. If she didn't know the basics of animal care, why was she here on a ranch?

Mulling that puzzling piece of information, he nodded and led the horse across the overgrown lawn to the barn. He'd been here a few times after Sally took sick, but she'd been too proud and stubborn to let him help her. When he'd heard she'd passed on, he regretted not insisting—or simply doing what needed to be done. He hadn't known she was that bad off.

Story of his life. Too little, too late. Don't notice what needs doing until after the fact.

Inside the large, red barn, which was newer and nicer than the old-style farmhouse, a testament to Sally's love of her animals, he led the horse into a stall and removed his rope.

"This should hold you for now." He stroked a gloved hand down the soft muzzle. "Stay put, little man."

When he left the barn, he took in the size and scope of Sally's stock. Wire pens squared off at least twenty acres of pasture that was dotted with a few shade trees and feed troughs. Another twenty acres spread to the north, while a double row of cottonwood and pecan and a few willows lined the narrow creek and circled a small pond.

Each of the pens within sight held some sort of critter, all of them perfectly useless-looking to him. Who would spend money on miniature goats, sheep, horses, and donkeys? Even the scrawny-necked chickens pecking the ground outside an elevated hen house had rock star haircuts and feathery feet. Did they lay eggs or jelly beans?

"Strange." But Sally had always been eccentric, especially in a county of genuine cattle ranchers. No one had taken her seriously. They had real animals. Hers were toys, a cute hobby.

Nate walked the short distance back to his truck, thinking of the animals and the redhead and those two little girls with the identical chocolate eyes and nearly black hair.

Who were they? What were they doing here?

Nate didn't know why, other being a neighborly sort, but he pulled down the rough, rutted driveway. Someone needed to get out the box blade and do some serious grading. A man could lose an eighteen wheeler in one of these potholes.

The redhead came outside. This time, the two little ones followed like ducklings. They were cuties. Like their mom.

That way lay danger, so he redirected his thinking. He was being a good neighbor. End of story.

"I put him in the stall and wired the latch. He won't escape again."

"Thank you. Sorry about running off on you like that. The babies were alone and..." She lifted a dirt-streaked shoulder and let the obvious slide as she offered a slender hand. "I'm Whitney Brookes."

"Whitney." He tried the name on for size and decided he liked it. Then, realizing he was still wearing gloves, Nate ripped one off and took her hand. His big paw swallowed hers and was a lot rougher. A lot. Hers felt like velvet. City girl. He had an instant flash of his ex-wife. If Whitney was anything like Alicia, she wouldn't last long on a ranch. "Nate Caldwell."

"Caldwell." An attractive frown dipped between her brown eyebrows. "As in the Caldwell Ranch?"

"Yes, ma'am. The Triple C. My brothers and sister own it, along with me."

"So we're neighbors."

I guess we are." He hadn't felt so tongue-tied since third grade when Mrs. Crandle made him stand in front of the class and explain why he'd let a garter snake loose in the girl's locker room. "You're taking over Sally's place?"

"I am."

Why did the first woman he'd found attractive in years have to become his neighbor? A neighbor he was already feeling sorry for. A neighbor whose house he'd have to drive past almost every day.

A tiny pair of arms encircled his leg. Relieved to have a distraction, he crouched down to eye level with the small beauty. "Hey, little one. You sure are pretty."

He'd almost said, "as pretty as a bay mare," but he caught himself in time to shut up. To his bafflement, women did not receive such compliments in the spirit in which they were given.

"That's Olivia." Whitney put her hand on the other toddler's back. The little girl leaned away from Nate, giving him the once over with eyes as big and dark as Oreos. "Miss Shy Bones here is Sophia."

"How do you tell them apart?"

She smiled a gentle mama's smile that spoke of her feelings for the twins as words never could. "Most of the time, I'm the only one who can. I just know."

The notion made him feel soft inside. Mamas and their babies. Watching them got to him. Not that he'd let on in front of his brothers or the ranch hands, but that's why he enjoyed working with the brood cows. They not only fed and nurtured their calves, they'd die fighting for them—and sometimes did. A human mama was even more ferocious.

Suddenly, he missed his mother with a pang as sharp as

a spur rowel. She'd been gone most of his life, and yet, the hurt and loss was always there.

He stood, and the twin, Olivia, latched onto his leg again.

Whitney laughed softly, another sound that made his heart squeeze. "I think she's taken with you."

He didn't know what to say to that. He liked kids but had missed the fatherhood train when Alicia miscarried and decided she was happy about that turn of events. Motherhood wasn't her gifting. Neither was ranch life with a bunch of smelly cowboys. That's what she'd said. Right before she'd driven off with another man. Her big city orthodontist.

That was seven years ago, and he'd not had the inclination to ride in the love rodeo since. Not even once.

"I made some iced tea," the redhead said. "Come in for a glass. It's the least I can do to repay your help."

He should leave. He had pregnant heifers to check and a gate to replace before the sun faded and he headed home. Connie, the Triple C's chief cook and housekeeper and everyone's surrogate mom, had promised enchiladas tonight, his favorite, and no one made the Mexican specialty better.

But instead of making his excuses, he said, "Sounds good."

Truth was, he was curious about Whitney Brookes and this farm. Not in a romantic way. He was done with that. Two strikes and he was not only out at the plate, he was out of the game. But he felt a responsibility as a neighbor and a Christian to make her welcome. And he couldn't help his curiosity. Who was she? What was she doing here? And where was the daddy to these pretty babies?

Whitney opened the old-style storm door—a window

on top and a screen on bottom—to let in the fresh air, and lifted first one and then the other child over the threshold.

Nate noticed her legs, smooth, tanned and shapely beneath rumpled, dirty shorts and long, bloody scratches. Nothing wrong with noticing. Christian or not, he was still a man, though he'd tried hard to put the longing for wife and kids behind him. He had the Triple C, and the hodgepodge family they'd made together was enough. Most of the time.

Removing his hat, he followed Whitney and her children into Sally's living room. The place was a mess. Boxes stacked here and there. Baby toys scattered over the couch and floor.

"You haven't been here long."

"No." Stepping around boxes, she moved into the kitchen. The old-style house separated the two rooms, and he followed Whitney through the disheveled living room into the kitchen. Two more boxes, one of them open and displaying a mismatch of plates, plastic bowls, and cups, rested on the short butcher block counter.

"I hadn't realized this property was for sale." He might have bought it if he'd known. The back of Sally's forty acres joined the Triple C, and they wouldn't mind adding this corner to their eleven thousand acres. Sally wouldn't sell, and they didn't push.

"It isn't. I inherited it. Sort of."

He blinked, surprised. "You're Sally's kin?"

One slender shoulder lifted. "I didn't know she existed until a few days ago. But apparently, Sally and my great-grandmother were double cousins and very close back in the day. According to her will, Sally had one closer relative, my distant cousin, Ronnie Flood, but she never liked him."

And Nate knew why. "So she left everything to you?"

"Crazy, huh? But a huge blessing to me and the girls. A real answer to prayer."

"Bet your cousin wasn't happy about that."

"I don't know. I've only seen him once or twice in my life." She glanced away and worried her bottom lip. Nate wondered why the mention of family bothered her. He could read it in her body language.

He remembered Ronnie, probably knew him better than she did. Nate certainly understood why Sally hadn't left her precious farm to the weasel of a man. Ronnie had come around Calypso one summer ostensibly to work for Sally. Turned out, the man was a mooch who borrowed off everyone, including him and his brothers, and likely skinned Sally for a good bit of cash before he split for parts unknown. He hoped the pretty redhead wasn't anything like her distant cousin.

2

At the mention of family, Whitney finished filling glasses with ice and tea. She refused to think about St. Louis and the family she'd left behind years ago. Regrets of that magnitude hurt too much.

Sophia patted her leg. "Mama. Mama."

"What, baby?" At two and a half, the girls loved to jabber, mostly to each other, but if they wanted something, the words came through loud and clear. At least, to her mama ears.

"You got da boo-boo. You weg is bweedin.'"

Whitney glanced at the spot where Sophia's finger rested. Her legs and arms had taken a beating from the gravel and briars, but she'd had no time to deal with the dirt in her hair or the wounds. Both babies had been awake and wailing when she'd gotten back to the house. "I'm okay."

"I get da bandaid." Sophia toddled off toward the still-empty bathroom, and Olivia, after a squinting squat to stare at her mother's knees, followed.

"You should go and take care of that." The cowboy stood

directly inside the kitchen door, gray hat in hand. Every time she looked at him, she got a funny, wobbly feeling inside. He seemed like a nice man, cordial and easy in his skin, so that he calmed her jittery nerves. Plus, he'd rounded up the stupid horse. And she had to admit, talking to an adult was a welcome change.

If she was honest, and she had no reason to be anything else at this point, she didn't know what to do now that she was here on the ranch. Nate Caldwell was clearly a cowboy with lots and lots of experience in raising animals. Though she didn't want to be dependent on anyone ever again, asking advice wasn't being dependent. Was it?

He had experience. She needed the help. He lived nearby. Would he?

She handed him a glass of fresh amber tea. "I guess I look pretty rough."

One side of his mouth tilted. "Wrangling a mighty steed like that one is hard work."

Whitney studied his rugged face. Was he teasing? She'd forgotten how to joke with a man, and flirting was out of the question. "It is to me."

Most of Sally's animals were small, but to her, they might as well be ten feet tall and weigh a ton. She'd lived her life in the suburbs, not in the country. Dogs and cats, even hamsters, she understood, but not farm animals. Especially strange little creatures like these. Sure, she'd gone to summer camp and *sort of* learned to ride a horse —a big one—but she'd never been responsible for their care.

She had to learn and she had to learn fast. Failure was not an option.

She shoved a stack of paperwork off the table and onto a

chair. The eat-in country kitchen wasn't big, and the cowboy seemed to take up a lot of room.

"Sit down if you'd like, Nate, and drink your tea. I'll be back in a minute after I wipe off some of this dirt and blood and check on the twins."

After firmly shutting the girls out of the bathroom where they'd been unrolling the toilet tissue as they jabbered, Whitney returned to the kitchen with a cleaner face and a handful of Band-Aids. Yes, she'd hurried. Not because she was attracted to the cowboy, but because he was in her house, and she wanted to be a good neighbor, especially considering the favor she needed.

She plopped the Band-Aids on the counter, opened several, and decorated her knees and shins.

"Snoopy?" The cowboy saluted her kneecaps with a half-empty tea glass and a wry expression. He had not, she noticed, moved from his spot by the kitchen door.

She had that effect on people, she supposed. They'd remain standing, so they could run away faster.

"Cures all boo-boos, even the imaginary ones."

Raising one arm like a chicken wing and twisting her head sharply to the side, Whitney attempted to assess the elbow damage.

"You'll never reach that." A very wide hand appeared in her peripheral vision and gently took hold of her elbow. "Let me help."

His voice was baritone warm and really close to her ear. Every cell in Whitney's body went on high alert at his surprisingly tender touch. As he gently dabbed the bloodied spot with a damp paper towel, her pulse gave a funny stutter.

She raised her eyes to watch him. The cowboy's focus

was on her injury, so she could stare her fill. And stare she did.

Brown-lashed eyes lifted. "Got any antibiotic ointment?"

Whitney quickly glanced down, pretending she hadn't been admiring his rugged face, the strong jaw, the firm lips, and the way he smelled of cotton shirt and clean air. A man's man. A woman's man, too. "No."

She sounded breathless. How ridiculous. She, who knew better, was already fighting an attraction to the first man she'd met. Men had been her downfall since she was sixteen. Would she never learn?

While she wrestled with all sorts of crazy emotions, Nate Caldwell cleaned and bandaged both her elbows like a pro.

When she found a sensible thought, she said, "Are you a doctor or something?"

Those firm lips curved. "Or something."

He released his hold and stepped back. "Snoopy's got you covered, but you probably should pick up some antibiotic cream for those scratches. Some are pretty deep."

"Sure. Thanks." She reached for her tea and swigged as she melted into a chair and searched for something to say besides, *you smell good.*

"Your ranch is the next one over, right? The one with the big cross timbers?"

He spun one of Sally's four chairs around and sat, tea glass dangling over the chair back. "Yes, ma'am. The cross timbers is the entrance to the main house where we live."

"You and your wife?"

"No wife. Not anymore. She left a few years back." Nate stared into his tea glass, expression serious. The divorce had hurt him. "My brother Ace and me live on the ranch now, but there's four of us kids. Brother Wyatt's in the military.

Emily lives in her own place on the ranch. She's a social worker, not a rancher."

"Just one sister?" Caldwell's place, from what little she'd seen in her efforts to find her way around, was enormous, and several homes dotted the landscape.

Nate started to say something else but shook his head and swigged the tea instead.

Whitney was curious about the reaction, but she didn't push. There were plenty of things she didn't want to discuss either.

The twins toddled in, and Olivia plopped a clean diaper in Nate's lap. "I wet."

"Olivia!" Whitney jumped up and swung her daughter into her arms. With an embarrassed grimace, she took the diaper from Nate. "Excuse me while I change her."

He set his glass on the table and started to rise. "I should go anyway."

Panic struck her. "No! I mean, please don't go yet. I want to ask you something."

Hoping she'd convinced him to wait, Whitney rushed down the narrow hallway to the room she'd designated as nursery. For now, she had their one, single crib set up, an onerous task that had seemed simple, but finding all those bolts and screws had taken forever. The rest of the room would wait. She'd sold most of her remaining items to get here. Not that she'd had much left. Thankfully, the girls still preferred to sleep together anyway.

When she returned to the cheery red kitchen, she found Sophia sitting at Nate's feet, rubbing the dust off his boots with her sock. She was barefooted again.

Whitney relocated both girls to the play drawer, a bottom cabinet she'd filled with harmless plastic toys, lids, and spoons. They loved to remove each item. Unfortunately, they'd yet to learn how to put them back.

"You've got your hands full."

"Twins are time-intensive."

"Do you have anyone to help with them?"

"If you mean the girls' father, no. We're not together." The stab of betrayal didn't hurt as much as it once had. "He left when they were born."

Whitney didn't know why she'd told him such a personal thing.

Nate frowned in disapproval. She liked him for that.

"Must have been rough on you, alone with two newborns."

The lost job, the eviction notices, the shelter smell of human bodies and bleach flashed through her memory.

He had no idea how hard, and she didn't want anyone to know.

"More than I care to remember." She pulled a length of hair over her shoulder and settled a tender gaze on her babies. "But they're worth everything."

"What about your mom and dad? I'd think grandparents would be crazy over twins."

That awful feeling of failure rose in her throat. Like a clutched hand cutting off her air supply, the string of failed relationships choked her. From her parents and grandparents to a myriad of ex-boyfriends. Failures, all. Her fault. She'd been the rebel who knew everything and didn't need anyone, especially her parents. How foolish she'd been.

Something was fundamentally wrong with a woman no one could love for long.

"No family." No family that wanted her, anyway.

She'd phoned her parents once when she was pregnant.

Mom had hung upon her. She wouldn't make that mistake again.

Tears burned at the back of her eyelids. She would not cry, not in front of this stranger, no matter how pleasant he was and how easy to talk to. She gulped a bracing swig of tea.

"I guess I brought up a bad subject. None of my business." He plunked the glass down again and rose. "It was good meeting you, neighbor. If I can help you in anyway, give me a call."

Whitney rose too, pulse hammering against her collarbone. "About that. Help, I mean."

He tilted his head, curious. "Yes?"

She didn't want to ask. She wanted to succeed on her own. Sally had. But Sally was born and raised with ranch animals.

She swallowed the last ounce of pride she'd been clinging to. "I can't lose this ranch."

He looked at her as if she made no sense. Which she didn't.

"What I'm saying is this, Nate. Sally left the ranch to me on the condition that I live in the house and successfully run the place for at least a year. When that year is over, I'm free to sell or do whatever."

His nostrils flared as if she'd said something distasteful. "A year's not that long."

"If I don't take proper care of the ranch, I lose it. If the animals get sick and die, I'm out. If they run away and get lost, like Clive wants to do, everything goes to Ronnie Flood." She stepped closer, ashamed of her desperation but praying like mad that she could convince him. "I'd like you to teach me about ranching. I'll pay you."

And do my best to ignore the tingling effect you have my skin.

Nate blinked, thunderstruck. "Me? Teach you?"

She nodded. Olivia and Sophia must have felt her anxiety because they toddled to her side and clung to her legs. Sophia started to whine. Reflexively, Whitney stroked the top of her silken hair.

"You live nearby. You could stop in whenever you have time, maybe first thing in the morning before you start your day."

"My day starts at five. Sometimes earlier."

"Whenever, then. I'll make it work." She was pleading now. "Come over whenever you have time. I don't even know what to feed them. Or how much. What if I make them flounder?"

His lips, those firm appealing lips, quivered. "You mean, founder?"

"See? I don't know enough to keep them alive for a whole year, and I have to. I can't lose this property. I can't."

But he was already shaking his head. "The Triple C is a huge enterprise. It keeps us all working dawn to dusk to take care of what we have and to generate a profit."

Sophia sniffled. Whitney wanted to do the same. Instead, she straightened her shoulders and nodded. "I understand. I'm sorry to impose."

Nate shifted on his boots, decidedly uncomfortable. She'd put him in a lousy spot. "I guess I could ask around for you, if you'd like, help you find a hired hand."

"You'd do that?"

"I could try, but I have to tell you, most cowboys think Sally's miniatures are a cute little hobby, not a livelihood."

Whitney didn't know if the ranch was profitable or not.

Not yet. But Sally had made a go of the place. "So, you're saying no self-respecting cowboy will work for me."

He winced, obviously sorry to be the bearer of bad news. "Like I said, ma'am, I'll ask around. Thank you for the tea."

Failure, once again. She couldn't even pay a man to hang around her.

NATE DIDN'T like feeling guilty. Lord knew, he'd felt that way often enough. But Whitney and her twins slapped a load on his back, and he carried it around all the rest of the day.

Late that evening as he parked inside the garage of the sprawling family ranch house, a two-story dormer, he considered what it would be like to have no family and to be the new kid in town the way Whitney was. He couldn't imagine. He'd always had the Triple C, plenty of family, and good friends all over Calypso County.

He felt sorry for her, but she'd irked him too. All that mattered to her was surviving the year. After that, she'd sell Sally's ranch for a nice profit and head back to wherever she'd come from. Probably a big city with lots of shopping malls.

He knew city girls when he met them. Especially when he married them. And why on earth was he thinking about marriage or his ex-wife in the same flash of brain wave as his new neighbor? But he knew why. She was pretty, personable, and too alone. She and those babies poked at the protective side of him. The one that had wanted family and kids.

Nate shook his head and muttered under his breath. The redhead was on his mind too much. Calypso was just a stop on her way to somewhere better.

Inside the house, the smell of spicy enchiladas greeted him, and Nate put his new neighbor out of his thoughts. He tossed his hat onto the hook in the mud room and shucked cow filthy boots. Connie Galindo, cook, housekeeper and surrogate mom, would chase him with a broom if he tracked manure on her floors.

Dad had built the sprawling structure thirty years ago, leaving the old original homestead to the ranch hands in order to accommodate four kids and extended family. Then Mom died, and a part of Dad died with her. Life went on, and Dad threw himself into work and kids, but till the day he graduated to heaven, Clint Caldwell never stopped mourning his bride.

Clint and Cori Caldwell, the Triple C.

Nate missed his parents with a yearning that never quite stopped. Working this ranch was his way of honoring them.

He entered the dining room and found Ace already seated at the table scooping enchiladas from the platter. The rectangular table for eight was emptier than usual tonight. Even Gilbert, the foreman who never missed a meal, was absent. Tonight, only Nate and Ace occupied the long, wooden expanse. Didn't seem right. A house this big needed family in it. But neither he nor Ace seemed inclined to make that happen.

Occasionally, Emily popped in for dinner, but she had her own house on the property, a home she'd once planned to fill with kids. Her dreams had died twice and since then, she'd focused on her work with someone else's children. Like her brothers, Emily had pulled the short straw in the love department.

"I started without you," Ace said without apology. "No lunch break. Already blessed the food."

Nate nodded as he took his place and began to eat, he on one side and Ace on the other. Ace was officially in charge of the Triple C, but Nate was the oldest. By birthright, he could have taken the head of the table. He never had. Neither would Ace. Dad belonged there.

"Cobbler for dessert."

Above his piled-high plate, Nate looked at his brother. Ace was the kind of cowboy women considered a heart throb—tall, lean, and loose-hipped. He had a smirky grin, plenty of wavy chestnut hair, and deep brown eyes that reminded Nate of those twin babies. The ones he didn't want to think about.

"Smelled it when I came through the kitchen."

He wondered what the redhead would think of Ace, but that idea made him restless. Ace was a heartbreaker. From the looks of her with those twins, Whitney didn't need that kind of complication.

Still, if the two lookers hooked up, he'd have no reason to think about her and her crazy offer. Imagine! Wanting to hire him to teach her about toy animals. He'd have been insulted if he didn't have a soft spot for anything four-legged.

He shoved a cheesy, spicy bite into his mouth, mulling, seeing the hope in Whitney's eyes fade away. Blue. Hers had been blue though the twins' were brown. Blue and troubled.

A man ought not to have such a powerful conscience.

Ace put down his fork and reached for the sour cream, but his gaze rested on Nate. "You're kinda quiet tonight. Got something on your mind?"

"I'm hungry."

"You're always hungry, but you usually talk while you're filling your belly. What's up? Trouble on the south range?"

Nate had spent most of his afternoon along the southern boundaries of the property with two day hands sorting cows. No trouble there. The trouble was in his heart.

"Saw five new calves. Two heifers and three bulls."

"That's good." Ace reached for a second helping. "Gilbert said someone's moving into the old Rogers's place. Did you notice anything when you drove by?"

Unless he rode horseback across a few thousand acres, Nate had to drive past the Rogers Ranch to reach the south side gate. Every single time.

"Yeah, I noticed." He really didn't want to talk about Whitney. Not until he had his head wrapped around his uncharacteristic thoughts. Attraction, that's what he felt, and he didn't want it. "Where is Gilbert anyway? He came to the house before I did."

Ace shrugged. "He'll show up when he smells supper."

As if they'd conjured him, Gilbert Tiger, a tall, wiry Seminole Indian, tromped in from the front of the house. "Nate knows about the new neighbors," he said. "He stopped by and wrangled a wild stallion. Tell him, Nate."

Gilbert snickered, and Nate shot him a sour look. The Seminole, their dad's army buddy, had lived on the Triple C before any of the siblings had been born. He was family of the heart.

"One of Sally's horses was loose. I rounded him up for her."

Gilbert pulled out a chair and sat down, suddenly more interested in the new neighbor than the meal he'd yet to eat. "Did you get her name?"

A slideshow of cinnamon hair and lightly tanned skin played behind his eyeballs. He recalled that moment when he'd bandaged her elbow. Her soft skin had him thinking crazy thoughts. Thoughts about holding her, about making promises, about keeping her and those twins safe and secure. "Whitney Brookes. She's got no help."

He didn't know why he'd added the last. But how could she make it on her own with two toddlers to look after and a ranch full of animals she knew nothing about.

"No one?" Gilbert helped himself to enchiladas and beans.

"No." Nate made a face. "She asked me to work for her."

Ace laughed. "I can see that now. Nate Caldwell milking three-foot-tall cows and branding itty bitty calves the size of house cats. Whoopee! Ride 'em, cowboy."

"My thoughts exactly." At the time, those *had* been his thoughts, along with uncharacteristic thoughts about the pretty mama and her twins. But all afternoon her request had weighed on him like a two-thousand-pound black angus. "I feel kind of sorry for her, though."

"Why? She bought a ranch. It's up to her to know what to do with it."

"I don't think it's that simple. She didn't buy the ranch. She inherited it." And she was desperate to keep it. Desperate, a bad place to be.

Ace screwed up his face in thought. "I didn't know Sally had kin except for that weasel, Ronnie something."

"Ronnie Flood." Weasel extraordinaire. "Whitney says she didn't even know Sally. Something about her great grandma and Sally being double cousins and best friends. No heirs, so she picked someone connected to her childhood friend."

"Not surprised. Sally always walked to her own drum beat." Ace shoved a forkful in his mouth and talked around it. "This Whitney, is she old? Young? Pretty?"

Nate huffed. Leave it to Ace to want to know those details. "Near our age, I guess. Thirties." He left the pretty part alone.

Connie swirled in from the kitchen toting that tantalizing peach cobbler on a pile of potholders. Her white Nikes made hushed sounds on the rock tile.

"You gonna love this cobbler, boys," she said in the accent Nate found both beautiful and comforting. "Fresh peaches from south Texas where we know how to grow 'em. Paco brought 'em in his truck, all himself, to the farmer market in Calypso."

The two brothers pushed their plates aside in their eagerness for the cobbler.

Did Whitney like peach cobbler?

Nate frowned at the aberrant thought. What was wrong with him today?

"Is there ice cream to go on top?" Ace asked.

"Sí. You think I make cobbler with no ice cream in the freezer?" Connie pretended insult but laughed, pleased at the men's eagerness.

That was Connie. Taking care of the Caldwells was what she loved. After Mom died, Clint Caldwell had been desperate for someone to help care for four young, grieving kids so he could work the ranch. Connie, with her thick Mexican accent and soft hands, had filled the bill. According to his father, she'd simply appeared at the front door one day, took baby Emily into her arms and the three boys under her wing, and never left.

Nate didn't know what any of them would have become without her. She'd loved them, taught them manners and Spanish, and shown them who Jesus was in the earthly spirit of one small Latina. He suspected she loved Clint

Caldwell as much as she loved his kids, but if Dad had known, he'd never let on.

Dishes clinked as the pie was passed around, and Connie offered up a carton of vanilla ice cream and a scoop. Then, as she did every night when "her boys" were settled, she took up her place at the table next to Nate and helped herself to the meal she'd cooked.

"I heard you talk about this new woman at Sally's ranch. Does she have a man?"

Nate didn't consider the ex much of a man. A real man wouldn't walk out on his woman and newborns.

While he pondered how much of Whitney's business to share, the ice cream melted down the sides of his cobbler. He dipped a fork into the decadence and white and peach swirled together.

"Has two little girls, twins. Just babies toddling around. Other than them, she's on her own."

There was the problem burning his insides more than the half cup of picante he'd doused onto the enchiladas. Whitney and her twins were all alone. She'd done her best to appear competent and determined after her tumble in the dirt, but her vulnerability had shown through.

"Alone? With two babies?" Connie's voice was pure sympathy and tenderness. "Is she from around here? She got people in Calypso?"

"No. I asked."

"Then, it is our Christian duty to be good neighbors. I will go tomorrow and introduce myself. *Sí.* I will take cobbler and ice cream. Emily should go too. They can be friends."

"Emily can't." Gilbert pointed a fork. "Court all day tomorrow in Clay City for her foster kid cases."

"You then." She jabbed a brown finger at Ace. "You busy tomorrow?"

Ace held up both hands. "Rotating pastures."

She turned calf eyes on Nate.

Sweet, fruity cobbler slid over his tongue and down the hatch to sizzle against the hot sauce.

No, no, not him. He held up both hands. "Promised Scott Donley a load of horse hay. After that, I gotta finish separating bulls and heifers on the south side."

"*Bueno.* That's close to Sally's ranch. We'll go and have a nice chat and invite her to church. Then you go to pasture."

Connie beamed as if she knew he'd love the idea. He didn't. He had work to do, even if he'd exaggerated a little when he'd told Whitney he was too busy. A rancher could always carve out a little time here and there. If he wanted to. And Nate didn't.

The little mama and her babies bothered him. Made him think about things best left alone.

But the woman legitimately needed a ranch hand, and he could probably find someone for her. Doing that didn't feel right either.

She'd asked *him.* But he couldn't. Wouldn't. He didn't need the complication of another woman in his life. A woman already planning her escape and she hadn't even been here a week! Not him. No way. The sweet mama would have to find some other lonesome cowboy.

Guilt pinched him. Was he being selfish?

Sally had left her in a mess. Her ex had left her in a mess. Nate knew about being left, about waking up in the dark to wonder why, and praying to understand God's plan even though he never had.

"Okay, Nate?" Connie's warm voice pushed into his dark thoughts.

Like everyone else, he'd hit some hard times, but he had a good life here on the Triple C. Maybe he was in a rut, and maybe he got lonely for female companionship sometimes, but so what? Life wasn't meant to be all fun and games. He knew his limitations, and he knew heartache. And he didn't want to go there anymore. No matter how appealing his new neighbor might be.

Connie patted his arm. "No greater commandment than to love our neighbors. It is God's will, Nate."

He knew Connie meant the *agape* God kind of love, not romance, but even hearing the word love in reference to the new neighbor made his insides jumpy.

He gestured with his fork. "Take Gilbert."

Connie waved the idea away. "Gilbert goes to the bull sale tomorrow. The woman knows you already. This will make it easier for her. We must show every kindness. This will honor our friend, Sally, and please God."

"Stop arguing with her, brother." Ace grinned at him. "She said you're going, and you know you will."

The cobbler settled like a brick in Nate's stomach. Ace was right. Connie was right too. Tomorrow he'd see the redhead again.

But he was not going to be the hired hand on that make-believe ranch for a woman as attractive as Whitney Brookes. No. He was not.

3

Whitney liked Calypso, a small town with businesses strung like a double row of colorful beads along either side of a two-lane main street. A mix of old and new, the buildings were mostly well kept, the sidewalks outside dotted with crepe myrtles and potted flowers. A few had awnings jutting out to create shade and shelter. A white-railed balcony extended from a slender two-story shop painted barn red, the calligraphied window proclaiming *Knits and Pearls*.

Traffic today consisted of a few cars and trucks slowing for the four way stop sign. If there was a stoplight in town, she'd yet to see it.

"We are definitely not in St. Louis anymore," she mumbled to the twins.

For the second time in three days, she drove to Hammond's Feed Store and parked outside. The last time she'd come here, she'd taken a quick walk around the store and, overwhelmed at the sheer unfamiliarity of absolutely everything, she'd rushed out before anyone could say a word to her.

Today, she'd do something productive. She had to. The feed left behind by whoever had been looking after the farm was about to run out. When she'd called him for instructions, Lawyer Leach said the rest was up to her. She had to prove herself worthy.

She hadn't been worthy of anything for a long time. But thank goodness, Sally had left money for supplies and to keep the farm going for a year if, according to the lawyer, Whitney budgeted properly. The trouble was, she didn't know what to expect in the way of budgeting, what kind of feed and supplies to buy, or even how much she'd need. Google might be useful if she had internet. Which she didn't. Was there even a library in this town?

She didn't know anything about country life.

Today she'd ask the feed store owner for advice. If Sally bought supplies for her ranch here, it stood to reason the store would have a record. She'd order whatever Sally had.

With a decided sniff, she straightened her shoulders, took the babies by the hands, and headed inside. Her olfactory glands reacted immediately. The place smelled like a barn mixed with some kind of chemical. Not unpleasant, really, just unfamiliar.

The handsome blond man she'd noticed from the parking lot during her first and completely unsuccessful visit was nowhere to be seen.

As had happened in the Dollar Saver grocery store, the twins attracted immediate attention and an older man in navy work pants hurried around the counter to squat beside them.

"Well, looky here. Twins, are they?" The man, his ball

cap displaying ears that would catch wind, grinned up at Whitney.

"Yes." She was wary of strangers in St. Louis, but everyone seemed so friendly in Calypso, and she didn't want to start off on the wrong foot. She was going to make a life in this town. Friendly was important. "Olivia has the red ribbons, and Sophia wears the pink."

"Well, ain't that handy?" He chucked Olivia under the chin. The toddler frowned at him. "Now, what can I do for you, ma'am? I don't think I got your name."

"Whitney Brookes. I inherited Sally Rogers's ranch." She squinted at the rusting metal sign on the back wall. "Are you Mr. Hammond?"

"Sure am. Me and my son run this establishment. So you're the one Sally left her babies to." He grinned when he said *babies*. "She always called them that. She sure doted on those animals."

"Yes, that would be me."

"I'll be dogged." He rounded the counter and hollered in the direction of what appeared to be a warehouse. "Matt! Get in here. Got a new customer, and she sure is pretty."

Whitney smiled. If everyone in Calypso treated her this well, she'd be a local in no time. Welcomed. Accepted. Two things she hadn't been in so long, she'd forgotten what they felt like.

A young man, handsome as a Nordic god, entered from the back room, scraping his Feed and Seed ball cap from his head when he saw her. He was a big, blond jock type, had likely played football in high school and now worked out at the gym to stay in shape. Or maybe he got that body from tossing around fifty-pound feed sacks. Nate probably did that too.

The thought of her reluctant neighbor brought her up short. She'd wrestled over his refusal all evening, but when morning had dawned after a miraculous night when both girls slept without waking, she'd put yesterday behind her and with it, Nate Caldwell.

She didn't need him. Oklahoma was farm and ranch land. There were plenty of cowboys and farm workers around. All she had to do was advertise, and she'd have a temporary employee in no time.

She smiled at the newcomer. "I'm Whitney Brookes."

"Yes, ma'am. Didn't you stop by the other day?"

Oh, lovely. He'd witnessed her near panic attack. "Briefly. I'd like to hire a temporary ranch hand. Someone to teach me the basics of running Sally's ranch. *My* ranch. Can you recommend someone?"

Matt looked uncomfortable. "Well, let's see. I guess you could post a notice on our bulletin board."

He gestured toward a four-by-four cork board inside the entrance, a board covered haphazardly in business cards, scribbled notes, and posters selling chickens, horses, and puppies.

Good. She could put an ad there. "I don't have a phone, but I guess applicants can apply in person."

She said *applicants* as if there would be plenty. She'd be thrilled with even one.

"Yes, ma'am. Everyone around here knows about Sally's little creatures."

"Great." She sucked in a breath, feeling accomplished, and outlined her need for feed. "Whatever Sally used."

Matt tapped the desk computer and clicked the mouse a few times. "Here we go. Her account is still in our system."

He rattled off several different feeds, vitamins, and other ranch-sounding items.

"Who gets what?"

He looked at her with a puzzled expression. "You don't know?"

She shook her head, miserable again. "Nothing. And I don't want to kill the poor creatures by feeding them the wrong thing."

"You do need a hired hand, don't you?"

"I do." Though the expense would cut deeply into Sally's nest egg.

"Tell you what." The clerk tapped a few more computer keys. "I'll fix up an order similar to the last one. That should hold you for a while."

"Are the directions on the bags?"

He looked as if he wanted to roll his eyes but was too polite to do so. "Some might be. Most won't be. But don't overfeed. That's a real problem, especially in those little bitty equines."

"How much is too much?" She sure hoped she hadn't been overfeeding.

Matt gazed at her another moment as if wondering what kind of ignorant city girl tried to run a ranch. Finally, he grabbed a pad and pen and scribbled a few notes.

"Here." He pushed the piece of paper across the counter. "This is a general guideline to get you started."

Whitney beamed and stuck the folded paper in her jeans pocket. "Thank you so much. This is really helpful."

"Want me to deliver that to your ranch, or are you taking it with you?"

Her ranch. Maybe she'd even change the name. Once she knew what she was doing. "You can deliver?"

"Yes, ma'am. Be happy to do that for you."

"That would be wonderful." The situation was looking up. She had guidelines and delivery and a brawny man to stack the heavy sacks in the barn.

"We'll get the order out today, if that works for you."

"Perfect."

As she turned to leave, twins in tow, Matt Hammond's voice followed. "Good luck with finding a ranch hand. I think you're going to need one."

WHITNEY STARED FIRST at the pile of bags and miscellaneous items stacked inside the red barn, then at the note the feed store clerk had given her. Clearly, he'd believed she knew more about animals than she did. She wanted to cry in abject frustration and helplessness. Break down right here on the barn floor, dirt, hay, manure and all, and give up.

But *give up* was no longer in her vocabulary. Not since she'd had the twins.

"Two pounds per hundred weight. Mostly forage," she muttered. "What does that *mean*?"

She scanned the rest of the barely decipherable note before sticking it back in her pocket. She needed a helper who knew what he or she was doing.

While she pondered her next move, Olivia and Sophia toddled after the furry chickens pecking the ground inside the barn. The flock of fowl apparently knew what to eat without any help. And except for Clive, captive in the barn, the horses, donkeys, goats, sheep, and cows seemed content munching the newly green grass. Was that what Matt meant by forage?

Asking meant another drive into town, but what choice did she have? Wearily, she herded the twins toward the house, but they were fascinated with the world this year in a way they hadn't been last year. They stopped every few feet to explore something. Sophia discovered a smattering of dandelion blossoms and squatted to investigate. Her wonder at the bright yellow flowers touched Whitney, and she crouched beside her daughter. The girls grew so fast, and Whitney had missed too much during those early days of distress and disruption.

"Pretty flower, Sophia." The dandelions had appeared overnight, a bit of golden magic, a splash of beauty.

The baby stroked the bloom with her index finger. "Fower."

Olivia, not to be ignored, plopped her diapered behind onto the grass. She ran her chubby hands through the barely-green blades, giggled, and flopped backwards, arms spread to either side. Sophia followed suit.

With a love so big she wondered how she could hold it, Whitney tickled each girl and relished their gurgling laughter. This was worth all she'd been through. Her babies, her girls, the loves of her life.

Stretching full length on the grass, she lifted each child in turn overhead and wiggled her until laughter rang out like music over the ranch.

A big truck rumbled into her driveway, stirring dust. Sitting up, a child on each thigh, Whitney watched Nate Caldwell's pickup stop near the barn.

A funny *kerthump* banged in her chest. She batted down the sudden thrill and focused on her goal. A home for the girls. A ranch hand for her.

Had Nate changed his mind? Would he teach her the

basics of animal care? Hope, that pesky emotion, sprang up as fast the dandelions.

The sturdy cowboy, muscles and all, leaped down from the truck and circled the hood to open the passenger door. A small, middle-aged woman slid with lithe ease to the ground and reached back inside. Nate wasn't married, and he and his companion weren't of the same generation, so who was this lady?

After standing each baby on her feet, Whitney got up from the grass and herded them out to meet the visitors.

Nate, all cowboy hat and boots and rugged good looks, toted a covered casserole dish while the woman carried a grocery bag.

"Howdy neighbor." Whitney hoped she sounded neighborly enough. "Change your mind?"

Nate scowled. "No."

She'd expected his response, but she was still disappointed.

The other woman extended her unfettered hand. "I am Consuelo Galindo. Call me Connie. I am the cook on the Triple C."

Nate made a growly noise. "She's a lot more than that."

Connie flashed him an affectionate, motherly look. "We have brought welcome gifts. You like peach cobbler? *Sí?*"

Whitney couldn't stop the huge grin that split her face. "Peach cobbler? For real? I haven't tasted homemade cobbler in...a long time."

Years, actually. Since before she'd run away to find a better life and met reality instead.

"*Sí,*" Connie said, a smile flashing on her dark face, "Pie and ice cream. These babies can eat ice cream, no?"

"Oh, yes. They *love* ice cream." Whitney gestured toward the house. "Come inside, please."

Delighted at the chance to meet neighbors, especially one as pleasant as Connie, and hopeful that she could sneak in a few questions to Nate about the feed issue, she lifted Sophia onto her hip.

Before she could reach down for Olivia, Nate had the toddler scooped into the crook of his elbow.

"Lead the way. I've got this one."

Something moved beneath her ribcage. Gratitude. Appreciation of the man. When had anyone helped her with the twins? "Thank you."

Once inside, she led her guests to the sunny country kitchen and found enough bowls to go around. They didn't match, but they were all she had.

As Connie chattered away about Calypso and the local evangelical congregation she and Nate attended, her brown hands dipped cobbler and ice cream into bowls.

"You and the babies come to church on Sunday. You meet Emily and all the others. They have good teachers for the nursery. The girls, they gonna love it. God is good."

At Connie's friendly jumble of words, Whitney smiled. "I've wondered about church. I haven't been a Christian long, but my faith is important."

"Good. Good. Nate will pick you up at nine sharp."

Nate glanced up as surprised as Whitney, but he didn't argue. Connie, apparently, reigned supreme at the Triple C.

"I can drive myself if you'll tell me where it is."

Connie stuck a bowl of cobbler in her hand and waved an ice cream scoop. "You come to Sunday dinner after. I cook a big meal. Nate will bring you."

"Oh, I couldn't impose."

Connie looked at her as if she was from another planet. "What is this impose?"

Nate took his bowl of cobbler and sat down at the table. Olivia, taken with the big man, lifted both arms in the universal sign for *pick me up*. He did, balancing her on one knee with a muscled forearm around her small waist.

Something went mushy in Whitney's insides when he shared a bite of his ice cream. Big man. Little child.

"Impose means Whitney thinks she'll be in the way." The cowboy wiped Olivia's face as if he fed ice cream to toddlers every day. "She thinks coming over for Sunday dinner would be too much trouble for us. For you."

Connie laughed a big hearty laugh that didn't fit her small, wiry form. "Sweet girl. This is what neighbors do. Emily and I need another woman to talk to. All these men. All over the ranch, I have men, men, men and only one girl who is seldom home. Come, you do me a big favor!"

Unexpected emotion clogged Whitney's throat. The woman was showing more kindness than she could possibly know. "Then, I accept. Thank you."

"Everybody has to eat, and I love to talk." Connie set a bowl of ice cream on the table and lifted Sophia onto her lap. "Too long since I fed a baby. My Caldwell boys, they no make babies. Maybe soon, though. I pray for good wives to come."

Nate cleared his throat and darted a quick glance at his housekeeper. She paid him no attention.

Whitney didn't know what to say, either, and focused on the dessert. "This is delicious, Connie. Did you make it yourself?"

"*Sí.* I teach you if you like."

"That would be wonderful."

A frown creased Connie's brow. "You no cook?"

"Enough to get by, but not like this. Pies and cobblers are kitchen magic."

"I teach you. Maybe you marry one of my boys. They eat a lot."

"Connie." Nate groaned. "For the love of Pete, Whitney just moved in. Don't start playing matchmaker. Remember your last disaster."

Whitney didn't know about the last one, but any romance for her was a disaster.

"That was nothing. Water under the bridge." Connie touched her nose to Sophia's and crossed her eyes, making the baby giggle.

Nate met Whitney's gaze, and they both smiled. A pleasant little butterfly took flight somewhere beneath her rib cage when he mouthed, "Sorry."

"No problem." Actually, it *was* a problem. She was thinking flirty thoughts about the cowboy, and that simply wouldn't do.

Connie slid ice cream into Sophia's bird mouth, dodged a grabby little hand, and kept talking. "You like flowers?"

"Love them. But I don't think Sally has any flower beds."

"She didn't. I try to give her some bulbs and seeds, but she say it's not her thing."

"It is mine." Or it used to be.

"That's why she has grass in her hair." Nate's comment was wry as he stared pointedly at the side of her head.

"Oh." Whitney batted at her mussed hair. "The girls found a dandelion, and we plopped down and..."

"Here. I'll get it." Nate leaned around Olivia and plucked out a few blades. He was close enough that his outdoorsy scent swirled around her.

Heat crawled up her neck and spread across her cheeks. Her interior butterfly flapped its wings. Hard.

What in the world?

Flustered, she blurted the first thing that came into her head. "How much feed should I be giving the animals?"

Nate blinked slowly as if he thought she might have a loose board in the attic. She did. Why else would she be in this situation?

"Which ones?"

She heaved a sigh of misery. "All of them."

Connie waved an empty spoon. "Go show her, Nate. I'll watch the *niñas*."

"You really don't know how to feed a few little cows and horses?" Nate asked.

"Or goats and chickens." She wagged her head from side to side. "I asked the man at the feed store and he gave me this." She dug in her pocket and handed Nate the scribbled note.

After a brief perusal, he got up from the table. "I don't know a lot about minis, but I'll have a look."

Thank you, Jesus!

Relief running like a fresh stream, Whitney followed the cowboy to the barn where she showed him the feed room. He ducked inside to study the sacks, the funny colored salt blocks, and the other supplies.

"You don't need much of this now. They'll mostly forage on pasture during the summer if you rotate the lots on a regular basis."

Forage meant pasture. Got it. "So I don't have to buy feed every month?"

"No. They mostly graze and do their own thing until winter when we supplement feed and good hay. Otherwise, minerals are important, and you need to keep the equine feet clean and trimmed. Worm them every couple of months."

More undecipherable language. "How do I do that...that foot and worm thing?"

He removed his hat and studied the brim, pensive for a few beats. "Taking care of a herd, no matter their size, requires knowledge, Whitney."

Thanks a lot, cowboy. Tell her something she didn't know.

"That's why I'm trying to hire someone to teach me," she said as patiently as she could manage. "If these animals die or I don't manage the ranch according to Sally's will, I lose everything. Hanging in here for the first year is crucial."

His nostrils flared in distaste. "I'm not for hire."

"I know. I know." In frustration, she ran a hand over her forehead, pushing hair away from her face.

"Your hair's real pretty." He shifted on his boots as if he didn't recognize his own words. "The color, I mean."

"Oh." Self-conscious, she touched the lock hanging over one shoulder. "Thank you. I like your-uh-boots." And your face and the creases at the corners of your mouth and the way you walk and talk.

He laughed, spun on those good-looking boots, and headed out to the corrals.

4

Nate looped his arms over the metal fence and propped a boot—the ones Whitney had admired—on a bottom rail. He didn't know what had come over him in the barn to make such a lame comment.

"But her hair *is* pretty," he muttered to the donkey snuffling his pant leg.

"Did you say something?"

He turned slowly, hiding his surprise that she'd followed. "Time to rotate pasture."

A frown appeared between her eyebrows. "How do I do that?"

"You really are a city girl, aren't you?"

"Born and raised."

Just as he feared. He was attracted to another one. Was he crazy or what?

With a sigh, Nate explained a few things about the animals, about rotating pens. He was here. Sharing information wasn't that big of a deal. She wasn't asking him to fall in love with her.

"I'll give you my cell number. You can call or text if you have a question."

He couldn't stop at her place every day. He was too busy. Well, not *that* busy, but she was too pretty and vulnerable. He was a sucker for vulnerable. Right now, he *really* wanted to touch that smooth, glossy red hair and tell her he'd take care of her animals...and her.

He needed to have his head examined.

"Can't. I don't have a phone." Pretty white teeth gnawed at her bottom lip.

Nate frowned. "You need a phone out here. What if something happened? You have little babies."

For some reason, his innocent remark got her back up. Her blue eyes got all shiny like clear glass.

"Don't you think I know that? Don't you think—?"

Her hands fisted at her sides. With a toss of that fascinating hair, she spun away and stomped back to the house.

Nate blew out a long, weary breath. He certainly had a way with women. Like always.

"A cell phone. Right. Idiot man. Do you think I'm completely stupid?" Probably. She sure didn't know anything about ranching.

Two hours after the Triple C visitors left, Whitney stewed over Nate's comment as she walked the nearest acreages counting fenced lots and animals. She carried a notebook and pen to make notes. Tomorrow she'd find the library, use the internet, and research...something.

With the twins down for their afternoon nap, she had time to start on a plan. The trouble was, she didn't know exactly how to start, especially when she couldn't stop thinking about Nate Caldwell.

His phone comment had been innocent. She'd overreacted, she supposed, out of embarrassment. He couldn't know how tight her budget was or her fear that she'd run out of money before she ran out of year. A cell phone was important, but not as important as feeding the twins and Sally's animals. Correction. *Her* animals. *Her* ranch.

She probably owed the man an apology.

In Oklahoma less than a week, and already she was making people dislike her.

With a sigh, she opened a gate and walked through the area counting goats. When she stopped to jot notes, the bearded billy tried to eat her shoelaces. She wrinkled her nose. "You need a bath."

Six of the little creatures must be females and, from the looks of them, every one was pregnant, a new worry to add to her list. What did one do with goat babies? And what if the mama goat had trouble? Was there a vet in town? And wouldn't vet care cost the moon?

As it was, two of the goats already showed signs of sickness. Mad cow disease maybe. Did goats get that? Costly or not, she'd have to locate a vet, another dent her budget, but the animals' survival was key to her own.

She jotted a note to ask at Hammond's Feed Store for a recommendation.

When she finished her rounds, after making sure all the animals had fresh water—even a complete novice knew animals required water—Whitney checked on the sleeping twins before heading to the barn and the feed bins. She wanted to stick notes on the various feeds so she wouldn't forget the things Nate had told her.

A red pickup truck slowed on the road in front of the farm house, stirring dust, and then turned down the awful excuse for a driveway. Whitney shielded her eyes from the sun and waited as the vehicle bumped and rattled over the potholes. Her visitor wasn't Nate, and she didn't know another soul except Lawyer Leach, and he drove a shiny black Lincoln.

"Who could that be?" She waited, watching and alert.

A tall stranger in hat and boots—another cowboy—hopped out of the truck, grinning as he moved in her direction. His walk was cocky, self-assured, and she couldn't decide if that was good or bad. Nate's walk was confident but not cocky. She liked to watch Nate walk.

"Are you Whitney?"

She took his measure, hesitant with a stranger. As Nate had reminded her, she was very alone out here. Without a phone. "Who's asking?"

He laughed, a friendly enough sound, but something about him bothered her. Maybe because he wasn't Nate.

"Call me L.T. I saw your ad at the Feed Store. Says you're looking for a man."

"Oh." A bubble of excitement replaced her momentary hesitation. Like the inheritance, this cowboy was probably the answer to her prayers! "Would you like to apply for the job?"

"Maybe." His grin never went away. "Why don't you show me around a little? I'd like to know what I'm getting into first."

"Of course." Whitney motioned toward the barn. "Obviously you know what that is."

"Uh-huh. You keep your feed and supplies in there?"

"Would you like to see where?"

"Sure." He dipped his chin, indicating for her to go ahead of him.

As she led the way, she felt his eyes on her. A frisson of concern rattled her nerve endings, but she chastised herself for being jumpy. She was unaccustomed to living in the country. That was all. The man had a legitimate reason for being here—she had advertised, after all—and she needed his help. She should be celebrating, not suspicious.

But inside the dim barn, Whitney grew even more nervous as she showed him around. He was nothing but polite, but she couldn't relax in his company. Not like she had with Nate.

She showed him the feed rooms and the smattering of equipment, none of which she understood in the least.

"I can't pay much, and the work is only part time." Whitney paused outside a stall that needed mucking. Maybe he'd turn her down. The thought cheered her but only until she came to her senses. She couldn't make this ranch work by herself. She needed his help.

He leaned a shoulder on a tall support post and let his gaze settle on her. "We'll work something out."

The cowboy wasn't bad looking. He was just...she was being ridiculous. There was nothing wrong with this guy except her wild imagination.

Whitney tamped down her nerves. "Do you have experience?"

He laughed softly. "Oh, yeah."

The hair at the back of Whitney's neck tingled.

Her eyes flashed to his. He was grinning again, watching her like a cat with a mouse. The overhead row of fluorescent lighting cast an eerie haze around him.

Maybe it wasn't her imagination. Maybe she should head right on out of this barn.

Suddenly, she wanted a cell phone more than she wanted her next breath.

"A gorgeous thing like you, alone out in the sticks, you definitely need a man to keep an eye on things." The grinning cowboy edged closer.

Whitney backed up and bumped into a stall door. The cowboy in front of her. Solid wood behind her. On her left, a wall. On her right, Clive in his stall, his shaggy head hanging... He'd be no help.

Her pulse picked up. She had to get out of here. The stench of L.T.'s cologne mixed with horse manure turned her stomach. So did L.T.

He scared her too.

Buying time to think, she pointed at the little horse.

"That's Clive. He likes to run away. Maybe you can help with that. If I hire you." *Which I won't. I don't like you.*

She was rattling, breathless, her nerves showing. Even if she was wrong, she wouldn't hire this guy. "What I really need is someone to teach me about ranching. It's a temporary job, part time for a few weeks, until I learn what I need to know. Really not much of a job at all. I don't think you'll want it."

"Let me be the judge of that." The cowboy stepped closer and lifted her hair from her shoulders. He rubbed it between his fingers. "I can teach you lots of things, pretty lady."

Whitney's pulse rattled like the tail of a diamondback. She understood his meaning all too clearly, and it didn't have a thing to do with raising livestock.

She jerked her head to one side to pull her hair free. "I'm

not interested in *lots of things*. Thanks for stopping by, but I don't need your services. Please leave. Now."

"Spunky. Chilly, too. Is that why you don't have a man? No one can handle you?" He stepped closer still, close enough that she could smell his breath mint.

She ducked, thinking she might squeeze under his arm. He caught her in an iron grip, one muscled arm around her back as he jerked her forward. He grabbed her chin, forced it up. In the next instance, his mouth came down on hers, hot and insistent, as his hands groped, touching her.

She wouldn't think about those hands. She could only think about escape.

Panic thundered in her chest.

She struggled, and the movement jiggled the stall door at her back. In a rush, it burst open, and she stumbled backwards, away from grabbing hands, away from his insistent mouth. She gasped a desperate breath and screamed. Dust motes and bits of straw swirled upward, and the scream ended in a cough.

L.T. laughed, but his eyes shot burning fury. "You put an ad out for a man, you should be ready for what you get. I don't mind the rough stuff if that's what you're into."

Frantically, Whitney searched the narrow stall for something, anything, to even the odds. There was nothing but straw and dirt.

He swaggered close again and shoved her against the back wall. She slapped him. He slapped her back.

This time there was no escape.

"Give these to Whitney when you pass by," Connie said.

"Tell her to plant them three times deeper than the bulb, and they will be beautiful next summer."

Nate was about to head to the south pasture anyway, so he took the plastic sack of iris bulbs without argument. He'd stop by tonight, after work, and drop them off. That way, he'd be in a hurry, have to rush to make it in time for supper, and would have an excuse to leave quickly if Whitney was still angry. Hand her the bag and hustle away.

Truth was, he didn't like that he'd upset his new neighbor. After his sister had reminded him that not everyone had money running out their ears the way he did, he recalled the state of Whitney's old car and the look of desperation in her eyes the first day he'd met her, and realized maybe she couldn't afford a phone.

When would he learn to keep his big opinionated mouth shut?

Dropping off the flower bulbs would be an apology of sorts, a peace offering.

As he passed her ranch, he noticed an unfamiliar pickup truck in Whitney's driveway. She had company. He started on past, then took his foot from the gas pedal and slowed. Maybe he should get this delivery business over with while someone else was around. Safe territory. Most people were more civil when others were present.

Might as well face her now, or he'd fret about it all day.

Shoving the shifter into reverse, he backed into the driveway, over the potholes, and parked on the grass in front of the house.

After exiting the truck, he started toward the porch. A scream spun him around.

His eyes scanned the area. First the pens. Had she been kicked or bitten? A horse's bite could destroy an arm.

Seeing no one, he aimed toward the barn, picking up speed as he drew closer and didn't hear another sound.

The big wooden door wasn't latched, so he shoved it open and stormed inside. She was in here somewhere. Maybe unconscious.

"Whitney! "He charged through the barn, searching stalls. He caught the slight sound of movement near Clive's stall. Fear gripped him. Had the hairy little monster injured her?

A stall door was open. Inside, Whitney struggled against a cowboy, one small hand pounding at the man while he grappled to control her.

In a red rage, Nate grabbed a handful of shirt and slung the cowboy against the cubicle wall. He drove a fist into the creep's belly. The cowboy went down with a loud oomph, arms curled over his gut.

Nate was so angry, he wanted to kick the jerk in the face and stomp him into the hay. He stood over the other man, glaring, fists tight and ready, huffing like a freight train.

"Nate." Whitney's voice was so small and shaky, it ripped his heart out of his chest.

He swiveled toward her. Her face was red, her mouth bleeding. A dark bruise had begun to form on one cheek.

Fighting not to kill the person who'd done that to her, Nate sucked in a long, hay-scented breath and tried to calm down."What's going on in here? Who is this guy?"

"I don't know. He-he…"

Nate grabbed the cowboy by the collar and yanked him to his feet. He glared at the other man's face.

"L.T.?" Now he was confused. "What are *you* doing here?"

"Caldwell." L.T. cradled his belly and groaned, but Nate

wasn't about to apologize. "This crazy broad. I answered her ad for a ranch hand, and she went nuts, threw herself on me."

Coupled with what he'd witnessed, one glance at Whitney and Nate knew L.T. was lying through his teeth. Her arms were crossed across her chest as if she was holding herself together. Her lips trembled. Tears pooled in her eyes. She was fighting the tears, trying to be tough, and losing.

Nate wanted to hold her.

Instead he tightened his grip on L.T.'s collar. "The bruise on her face and that bloody lip say different."

"So she likes it rough. What can I say?" The ingratiating creep had the audacity to grin. "Come on, Caldwell. You know the score."

The score? The score! As if Whitney was nothing but a game?

The anger grew hotter until Nate thought the top of his head would blow.

"Never did like you much." Teeth tight as his fists, he leaned into L.T.'s face. "You're going to jail." He slid a glance toward Whitney. "My cell's in the truck, Whitney. Get it and call 9-1-1."

The grin slid from the cowboy's face. "Hey, now, I didn't mean no harm. A little kiss or two is nothing to make a big scene over."

Whitney's fingers circled Nate's arm. "No charges, Nate. I just want him gone."

He could feel her shaking and got mad all over again. "Not a good plan. Call. The sheriff is a friend of mine."

"No. Please." A fat tear flooded one of Whitney's blue eyes and tumbled overboard. Her voice dropped to a pleading whisper. "Please, Nate. No police."

He relaxed his hold on L.T.'s shirt but kept him trapped against the wall.

"You positive?" He didn't agree, but it was her call to make.

L.T. made a move as if to ease around him. Nate caught his shoulder and shoved him back against the wall. Boards rattled. The other cowboy was taller, but Nate had a few pounds on him. "I didn't say you could leave."

Jenkins's face darkened, and his eyes shot pure venom, but he didn't argue.

"I'm positive. This is humiliating enough, and I'm new in this town," Whitney said. "I don't want people to think I'm a troublemaker."

"You heard the lady, Caldwell. She wants no trouble, and neither do I." L.T. bent, grabbed his hat from the dirty floor, and shoved it on his head. Straw drizzled down onto his western shirt. He plowed a shoulder against Nate's. "I'm out of here."

Nate didn't budge. Not yet. He wanted to make one thing very clear. "Make sure you don't come back."

There was a momentary stare down before Nate stepped aside and let the other cowboy walk away. When he heard the barn door slam, he turned to Whitney. "You okay?"

She ducked her head, wouldn't meet his eyes. "Yes."

He didn't believe her. She was embarrassed, shaken, and that bruise grew darker every second. Carefully, gently, Nate touched her cheek. "Let's get some ice on that."

She nodded, face flaming red and hot against his fingers. She licked her bloody lip and murmured, "My girls are alone."

His heart pinched. Her first thought had not been for herself, but for her babies. "Go."

As she loped out of the barn, Nate followed as far as the driveway to be sure L.T. was long gone. He stood outside for a couple of minutes, listening until the engine noise faded into the cloudy afternoon.

L.T. Jenkins was a strutting rooster and a second-rate ranch hand, but Nate had never expected something like this. What if L.T. returned when Nate wasn't here?

He dragged a hand down his face, contemplating the new problem dropped in his lap. What if he hadn't stopped? What if he'd waited until after work to deliver the flower bulbs? He couldn't think about what might have happened. What would certainly have happened if he hadn't shown up when he did.

God had sent him in the nick of time. He glanced heavenward. *Thank you.*

Whitney was alone, and she'd placed that ridiculous notice at the feed store. He'd read it, but did it worry him at the time? Not one iota.

Nate huffed a frustrated sigh. Story of his life. Never see the problem until it was too late. But now that he did, he could fix it before every hairy-legged cowboy who knew one end of a cow from the other showed up to *help* the pretty single woman who didn't know a thing about ranching.

With a groan, he understood what he had to do. The trouble was, he liked the idea too much. He liked *her* too much. When he'd seen L.T. pawing at her, he'd had thoughts no Christian man should have. Predatory thoughts. Caveman thoughts.

Dad and Connie had raised him to be a gentleman who treated women with respect and appreciation. He couldn't abide less from another man. Anyone who drove up that road had better have good intentions, or they'd answer to him.

Because no matter how inconvenient it was, no matter how busy he might be, he wasn't the kind of man who could walk away when someone needed him. He might fail—had plenty of times—but he'd fail trying.

He flexed his punching hand and stepped onto the porch. Whether he liked the idea or not, it was time to tell Whitney she had herself a ranch hand.

5

Hands shaking, Whitney took a dish towel from a kitchen drawer and moved to the refrigerator. The twins still slept, unaware, thank the Lord, of the drama in the barn.

Nate stood in the kitchen doorway, glowering like a mad bull about to charge. She wasn't sure if he was mad at her or mad at the kissing creep.

If Nate hadn't arrived when he had...A shudder earth-quaked down her spine at the memory. Of the lecherous cowboy, of begin trapped, of feeling helpless.

"I guess I asked for that," she murmured.

"What are you talking about?" His words were more barked than spoken.

"The sign at the feed store."

His scowl only deepened. "Don't be stupid."

Stupid. That sounded about right. Stupid and, in this moment, more grateful than she knew how to express.

In all her adult life, Whitney had never had anyone come to her rescue. She couldn't decide if she loved the feeling or hated it. She didn't want to be needy. After learning the hard way not to depend on a man, she was determined to stand on her own two feet. The incident in the barn only cemented the lessons she'd learned in the last few years—her own two feet weren't always sturdy enough.

"I don't think I've said thank you." Her voice sounded as wimpy and watery as she felt.

He crossed the room and took the towel from her hands —hands that wouldn't stop trembling—and growled, "Sit down before you fall down."

She stiffened. "I'm fine."

"Duly noted, but I can make an ice pack. Had plenty of opportunities working on a ranch." Nate put a strong hand on her shoulder and guided her to the chair. With a gentle push, he set her down. Having something solid under her wobbly knees felt good. He was right. Any second now, she might have slithered to the floor like a limp noodle. But giving in to the fear and vulnerability was akin to giving up, and she couldn't do either. Not with two babies to support.

A noise had her swiveling her head toward the hallway. "I think the twins are waking."

His back turned, Nate glanced at her over one very broad shoulder. "Take care of you first. They sound okay. You're not."

He was right about that, even though she didn't want to admit it.

From the back room, one of the twins, Olivia, she thought, jabbered to the other. Sophia was probably still napping, but knowing her dominant daughter, Olivia would have her sister awake in seconds.

Nate filled the towel with ice cubes, then pressed the compress gently against her face and lip. He hunkered down beside her, eye to eye. His were filled with compassion. Not anger at her stupidity. Compassion.

Something inside Whitney melted. Relieved tears pushed at the back of her eyeballs. Nate was upset *for* her, not *at* her. He wasn't mad.

She didn't know why his opinion mattered so much, but it did.

For several beats, the cowboy studied her face while her heart did funny jumping jacks. She could feel him breathe, see the golden marbling in his brown eyes.

Slowly, relief gave way to attraction.

At least for her. Maybe for him. It had been so long since she'd even considered a man's appeal, she wasn't sure.

This was ridiculous. Foolish. Dangerous. She needed a ranch hand, not a boyfriend. But oh my, he was one sweet cowboy.

Almost tenderly, he stroked the back of his hand over her hair and double tapped a knuckle beneath her chin. A friendly, *keep your chin-up* reminder, not a come on, and entirely different from the other cowboy's invasion of her personal space.

She was tempted to lean into his sturdy, comforting strength. She didn't, of course. Couldn't. Giving in to moments of weakness had been her downfall.

When she thought she might lean anyway, if only for a minute, he took her hand, pressed it onto the ice pack and then disappeared down the narrow hall, leaving her to examine the troubling emotions Nate Caldwell stirred inside her.

Nate was a salt-of-the-earth kind of man people lauded as solid and dependable and good at heart. It had been so long since she'd allowed a man to penetrate her thoughts, she didn't trust her judgment. She barely knew him, but that didn't stop her from wondering why his wife had left him. Why any woman wouldn't want Nate Caldwell.

From the nursery, she heard baby talk mixed with Nate's deep rumble. The twins giggled, and the cowboy's soft chuckle responded. Whitney stilled, straining to listen to the sweet, sweet sound. Baby laughter was the music of heaven.

Melting ice slid down her cheek and plopped fat drops onto her blouse. She refolded the towel and pressed it back into place as she pondered her neighbor. Was he God sent? Or was her neediness overshadowing her common sense?

"Incoming princess times two!" Boots thudded against wood floors as a smiling Nate re-entered the kitchen with a sleepy-eyed toddler in each powerful arm.

Sophia dug a tiny fist against one eye and yawned.

Olivia, pony-tails askew, patted Nate's chest and demanded, "Dink. Dink."

He shot a helpless look at Whitney. "I don't speak toddler too well."

"She wants her sippy cup." Whitney rose and took two plastic training cups from the cabinet. "It's our after nap routine. Sippy cup, fresh diaper, and then a little snack."

He grimaced. "I thought they felt a little damp."

While she smiled at his reaction, Nate settled in a chair and let the twins wiggle to the floor. Whitney handed over the cups, and each baby balanced a tiny hand on one of Nate's knees while gulping water. He rested a big, rough rancher's hand on each teeny shoulder, steadying them.

The picture stabbed Whitney right in the chest. They'd had no man, other than strangers in supermarkets, give them any attention. They were mesmerized by the cowboy.

If she wasn't careful, she'd be feeling the same.

BRIGHT and early the next morning, Whitney rose with the chickens. Literally. Every day at dawn, while gray shadows embraced the land and most humans still dozed, a red speckled rooster, a Polish, according to Sally's haphazard notes, with a wild feathered hair-do, stood on top of the chicken house and crowed as if he weighed five hundred pounds instead of two. And every morning, Whitney contemplated chicken soup.

This pink-and-gold sunrise, however, she was on a mission to be organized and ready for action when Nate arrived. As bad as yesterday had been, Nate had made it made better when he'd agreed to be her teacher. She didn't know why he'd changed his mind. Must have been pity. He didn't appear to like being around her that much, but whatever his reasons, she'd slept better last night knowing Nate would be stopping by on a regular basis. Now maybe she had a realistic shot at making a long-term success of her inheritance.

His offer to help had come with such reservation on his part that she'd expected him to jump in that big four-wheel-drive truck and spew dust all over her house as he made his escape. He hadn't though. Stetson in hand, he'd let her use his cell to call the feed store and have the troublesome note taken down. Then, he'd promised to teach her "the ropes" of basic ranching and animal care. And if she'd groveled and simpered in gratitude, she wasn't sorry. She needed him.

Even though ranching was scary and about as far out of her comfort zone as hiking the Himalayas with a polar bear, this was her best chance at making a good life for her little family. Her last chance. If she failed, the future looked too grim to think about.

She would learn, work hard, succeed. She had to.

Dressed and fueled with coffee and yogurt, she peeked at the girls one last time and, satisfied they'd sleep another hour, headed outside to water the stock. She'd read through one of Sally's notebooks last night, not that it had helped much. Sally had her own brand of undecipherable shorthand.

By the time the twins awoke and Whitney went inside to prepare their breakfast, Nate still had not arrived.

"Maybe he changed his mind." The thought depressed her. Apparently, Olivia wasn't thrilled either because she was fussy this morning, hanging on Whitney's leg and whining.

Whitney handed her a piece of banana while she finished scrambling eggs. That seemed to do the trick for now.

After breakfast and dressing the twins, Nate still hadn't arrived, so she headed back outside. The girls followed like baby ducks in their yellow shirts and black yoga pants.

Having them near the animals while she worked worried her, but what choice did she have? She had no playpen, and even if she did, the girls would crawl right over the top. Olivia was a champion at that little game, and Sophia was only too happy to follow her sister's lead.

Whitney looked around the barnyard for a safe place for them and found none.

"Babies and running a ranch don't mix." When both girls looked up at her with heart-melting brown eyes, she went to her knees for a hug. They smelled good, like baby lotion and bananas. Olivia was over her snit. Mild-tempered

Sophia babbled something about puppies, her name for every animal on the place.

By ten o'clock, she'd given up on Nate. The goats were baaing at her from their tightly structured fence, insisting on...something. One hairy little nanny tried her best to twist her head through a small opening in the wire panel. Funny little animals. Cute, too. She could get used to goats.

With the girls toddling at her side, Whitney carried a bucket of grain to the gate. Metal clanged as she stepped inside the pen. At the noise, all six goats fled in terror. Four nannies collapsed in a heap as if she'd shot them.

They'd done the same thing yesterday. At first she hadn't worried too much. What did she know about goats? But two days in a row? Something had to be wrong. What if they all died? What if these cute, silly creatures caused her to lose this ranch?

Panic shot through her veins. "Get up, goats. Get up."

She ran to help as each one struggled to her feet. When she approached, shooing them like chickens in her effort to encourage, they tipped over again, legs straight out as if rigor mortis had already set in.

Hand to her mouth, she watched in horror as the animals finally recovered and staggered to a wobbly stand. "They're sick. They're dying. I've fed them the wrong thing, and they're all going to die."

She stared down into the bucket of feed, reluctant to give them more. The grain looked okay. She sniffed it. It smelled okay, too. The bucketful was fresh from the bags Matt Hammond had delivered a couple of days ago.

Could that be the problem? Had Matt unintentionally sold her a batch of bad feed? Poisoned feed? Hadn't she seen that once on a horse movie? Moldy feed could kill a horse. Maybe it killed goats, too. Was this moldy?

The daddy goat crowded in as if to butt her. She stomped her foot to shoo him away...and to her horror, he collapsed in a cloud of dust at her feet.

That awful feeling of failure swamped her, drowning her again.

"I've got to find a vet." In a panic, she grabbed the twins and hurried toward the house for her car keys at the exact moment Nate's big truck wheeled into the drive. "Thank you, Lord!"

Leaving the babies with their toys on the front porch where she could see them, she spun and raced down the driveway, leaping over potholes. "Nate. Nate!"

Nate slammed out of his truck and swung in a three-sixty, searching the surroundings as if he was some sort of solider on a mission. "What's wrong? L.T.? Is he back?"

Whitney skidded to a stop in front of him, panting like a puppy. "The goats. They're dying."

"Dying?" One look at her face must have convinced him she was serious. With long, confident strides, Nate hustled to the goat pens and went inside. Whitney followed.

"They look okay to me." He stood, hands on hips, studying the small herd. The word *good-looking* flickered behind her eyelids at least ten times, like a flashing neon sign. Boots wide, hat low, a real cowboy. Strong, a little sexy, a lot manly.

She had to tear her gaze away to think straight. The topic was dying goats not her completely inappropriate responses to the rancher.

"One minute they're okay and the next they collapse." She started toward the nearest goat, patting her hands in what she thought would be an encouraging greeting. The little nanny bolted away, short tail aflutter.

After three steps, the animal fell over in a dead faint. Legs stiff and straight. Pot belly pooching out.

Whitney fought back a cry. "See? Something is terribly wrong. Do you think I bought bad feed? Maybe they ate something poison. Call your vet. Do something. I can't lose these goats."

Whitney realized then that Nate had gone strangely quiet. A bad, bad sign. He leaned against the panel fence, head down, hat tipped even lower to cover his face. He didn't want to be the bearer of bad news.

"I've killed them, haven't I? Go ahead and tell me the truth. I can handle it." A lie, of course. She could not handle losing the home her daughters needed.

A goat baa-ed. A cow mooed, and the chickens fluttered and clucked. Inside the barn, Clive, the runaway stallion, hollered at the top of his tiny lungs, sure he was starving to death in a stall filled with hay.

Whitney wanted to holler too. Life kept lifting her up to punch her face and knock her back down.

"Nate?"

He looked at her then, and she realized he wasn't in despair. He was trying not to laugh! His shoulders shook with contained mirth.

She stiffened like the legs of her dying goats. "This is not a laughing matter. Not unless you're trying to run me out of business."

The thought took root. Nate didn't approve of her miniature critters. He didn't consider them real livestock. And her land *did* back up to his. Maybe he'd like to see her fail.

No, that didn't make sense. He'd offered his help. He'd

rescued her from that cowboy cretin, and he was tender with the twins. Tender with her, too, if she'd admit it.

The telltale quiver around his mouth said Nate was not the least insulted by her accusation.

"Whitney, come here." He dumped the feed into a trough, flipped the empty bucket upside down, and patted the bottom. "Sit. Lesson one."

She shot a glance toward the porch. Side by side like matching dolls, the twins happily pushed a pink shopping cart loaded with toys around the flat wooden surface. Confident they were safe, she perched on the bucket.

The billy goat butted at Nate's back. The cowboy gave the animal a push and stomped his boot. Billy fell over dead. At least, he looked dead to Whitney.

"Shouldn't we call a vet?"

"I'm the closest thing to a vet you'll find around Calypso."

He was? "Then what is *wrong* with my goats?"

"Nothing." He hunkered down on the toes of his boots next to her bucket and picked up a piece of straw.

"Nothing? But they pass out, and their legs stiffen like road kill."

"Goats come in more than one variety. Yours are fainting goats."

"Fainting goats? You're joking." His mildly amused expression said he wasn't. Whitney leaned away, incredulous. "No way? They do this on purpose?"

"I don't know about purpose, but they're born this way. The fancy word for it is myotonic. When they're startled or excited, their muscles stiffen, and they collapse for a few seconds. Then they hop up and everything's fine."

"Fainting goats?"

Nate grinned. "Yep."

Whitney slapped a hand on top of her head and laughed.

"Fainting goats." She couldn't believe it. She hadn't killed them. They weren't poisoned. They were just doing what fainting goats are supposed to do.

To prove to herself that Nate was right, she stomped her foot. And Billy collapsed again. She giggled. "They're not hurt or sick?"

"Not at all. They're normal fainting goats."

The idea that there was anything normal about a goat that fainted was so ridiculous and such an incredible relief, Whitney began to laugh. And that made Nate laugh. Pretty soon, their laughter rang out over the animals' pens louder than any rooster crow or donkey bray.

He pointed the straw at her. "You thought they were dying."

Hand against her giggling mouth, she nodded. "I did!"

Nate laughed so hard, he lost his balance and tumped backwards into the dirt. When he yelped, six goats fell over in a faint.

Whitney hooped with laughter, pointing at him as tears flowed from her eyes. Tears of relief. Tears of pure mirth such as she hadn't enjoyed in months and months. Maybe years.

Hat off, brown hair glinting shades of gold and honey in the morning sun, and face crinkled in delight, Nate reached out and tugged at her arm, pushing the bucket with his foot. "If we're all fainting—"

In the next instant, Whitney was sitting in the dirt next to the broad-shouldered cowboy. At the clatter of noise, every single goat went down in a faint. And the whooping laughter commenced all over again.

When they finally got themselves under control and the goats were back up and hopping around the pen on stiff legs, tails happily aflutter, Nate rose and pulled her up with him. They stood facing each other, not too close but closer than virtual strangers usually do, and simply grinned.

Something warm and pleasant splashed in the center of Whitney's heart, in that place she'd closed off over three years ago.

Dust and country air and the smell of barnyard swirled in the atmosphere right along with camaraderie and laughter. She smiled, tremulously, grateful for a man who could make her laugh and forget her troubles even for a few minutes.

She glanced toward the house.

Nate followed her gaze, dusting his hat back and forth across his jean-clad thigh. "The twins are still playing, safe and happy. I've been watching."

There he went again. This man took *neighborly* to whole new level. During and since the awful time with her ex, the nearest thing to a good neighbor she'd had was the landlord who'd helped her pack the Subaru after she'd been evicted.

Nate started toward the gate and then stopped, one hand on the latch. "Before I forget..."He removed a small cell phone from a pearl-snapped shirt pocket and held it out.

"What's this?"

"A cell phone."

"I know that. I'm not that dumb."

"You're not dumb at all, but you are a woman alone." When she began to shake her head, he said, "Don't get your back up. You need a phone."

"You bought me a phone?"

"We had an extra lying around for the hands. A ranch phone. Text and talk only. Not that expensive. Take it."

Was he telling the truth or offering charity? "I can't accept this. I can't—"

His look could quell a charging elephant. "Look, consider it a loaner until you get your own. You're doing me a favor. Otherwise, I won't sleep at night wondering what idiot you've let in your barn."

The reminder put starch in her spine. And here she'd been having sugary thoughts about him. "Thank you for throwing that in my face."

He huffed. "Just take the phone, okay? If not for your own safety, for theirs." He shot a pointed look toward the twins.

That was her undoing. Anything for her babies. He was right, after all, though pushy for insisting. She was being proud and stubborn, and she knew very well that pride led to a fall hard enough to break a bone. She couldn't afford to tumble any farther. The next time would kill her.

She held out her hand. "I'll pay the bill."

Nate crammed his hat back onto this head. "Fine."

He shoved the gate open and held it for her pass through. The laughter was gone, and she realized she'd caused the rift, maybe hurt his feelings.

The rest of their time together was not nearly as much fun.

6

N ate wiped sweat from his brow and looked at the sky, hoping for rain. So far, they'd had the driest September he could remember, and pasture grass begged for moisture.

He dismounted, leaving his buckskin gelding ground tied near the moveable chute they'd set up in the south pasture. Uncle Buck was a fine cutting horse who knew his job was over for the moment. Bawling calves lined the chute as cowboys guided them into the head gate to be wormed and vaccinated.

Carrying the syringe kit he'd pulled from Uncle Buck's saddle bag, Nate climbed onto one side of the gate. Gilbert rode the other side, while day hands pushed the calves through, separating bulls from heifers as they went.

The Triple C produced top-of-the-line Angus beef, and Nate made sure every animal was in superior condition. The day-to-day grind was dirty, noisy work, but he loved it. Give him the camaraderie with the other cowboys, the animals, and the outdoors over working the books and fretting about the budget, the market, and feed prices any day. He didn't even mind the hot, sweaty hay season when they put up tons and tons of round bales for winter and filled barns with protein-laden Bermuda for the horses.

Gilbert, dark skin sweating as much as Nate's, hollered across the gate. "How you doing with our new neighbor?"

The new neighbor. Yeah. As if she was ever far from his thoughts. Whitney had been the talk of the Triple C supper table all week. Once Emily heard about her, she'd rushed right over for an introduction that had turned into an entire evening with the newcomer. His sister liked her. With Connie singing her praises and dropping hints to the single Caldwell men, the talk grew a tad uncomfortable at times.

"She's all right."

"Hey boss." Beck, one of the day hands who looked too pretty to be a working cowboy, grinned at him from inside the chute. "Heard you were cowboying over there."

Nate shot a look at Gilbert. "You old gossip."

Gilbert just grinned.

"So it's true?" Beck guided a frisky calf toward the head gate and shook his head. "Never thought I'd see the day a Caldwell would ride herd on toy cows and horses."

Every cowboy within earshot guffawed. One of them hollered, "She must be a real looker."

She was. But that was beside the point. He was doing the woman a kindness, being neighborly. "Cut it out, boys."

"Ah, Nate, they don't mean any harm." Gilbert shot wormer down a calf's throat while Nate administered the inoculation.

In seconds, Nate released the head gate in a loud clatter of metal, and the calf burst out into the open pasture, bucking, kicking, and bawling for its mama.

"I know they don't." He was being oversensitive about Whitney, and he didn't understand why. Teasing was the cowboy way. If they couldn't rib each other about something, be it a woman, a horse, a mistake, or their boot size, they weren't happy. If there was one thing the Triple C prided itself on, it was a congenial work atmosphere.

The atmosphere at Whitney's place was pretty congenial too. He had no complaints. He still chuckled over the fainting goats. When he'd told Connie, she'd laughed but sympathized, and then bossed him, as usual. "Treat that sweet girl good."

He knew what Connie was up to, and it wouldn't work. He liked Whitney, but he was not getting involved. Not in the way Connie had in mind.

Still, Whitney made mighty good omelets from those little bitty chicken eggs, and he'd never known a woman so eager to learn. Dirt, manure, or cantankerous critters, she didn't back away from anything. When one of the little donkeys had kicked her in the knee, she'd gone down, then popped right back up.

She was gritty. He'd give her that. And those two little girls with their dark ponytails and big eyes were endlessly entertaining.

Less than a week in and he found himself rising earlier and earlier to get to her place. He rationalized that Whitney needed all the time he could give her. His actions had nothing to do with the thoughts Connie put in his head, thoughts that shouldn't be there.

"Nate! Wake up, man. We got three more calves in the chute."

At Gilbert's shout, Nate jerked his attention back to the job, embarrassed to be caught daydreaming. A few of the cowboys snickered as if they suspected where his mind had gone. Not that they could possibly know how often Whitney occupied his thoughts, but he'd better be careful. He didn't need the whole bunch of bunkhouse bozos giving him a hard time.

He continued through the motions with the vaccinations. He'd given the shots so often, he could properly inject a calf in his sleep.

"Hey, Boss, look yonder."

Nate followed Beck's line of sight, squinting. A frisson of concern nagged at the back of his brain. "That's smoke, boys."

He'd no more than gotten the words out than Ace's black Ford F-450 came over the horizon and skidded to a stop. Nate's long-legged brother hit the ground running. Dust and grass swirled into the dry air, and cows and calves scattered like bobwhite quail.

"Looks like fire, men. You about done here?"

Beck slapped the rear of the final calf. "One more."

"Good. See you there." Without further conversation, Ace galloped back to his truck and shot off across the pasture, the big Ford bucking and bouncing like a wild bronc.

Nate and Gilbert exchanged knowing looks. Fire was never good. With the air so dry and dozens of new calves and expectant mamas scattered over the massive ranch, they had to act fast. Wildfire was a dangerous business on grasslands.

In minutes, the final calf was worked. Nate hollered to Beck and the other three remaining cowhands. "Leave this. We'll clean up later."

He tossed his equipment into Uncle Buck's bags and

leaped into the saddle. The other men mounted up, too, and they raced toward the growing tornado of smoke.

They'd traveled a mile seeing only smoke before the flames came into sight, a sure sign of how massive the fire must be. Through gates and gullies, across creeks and pastures, Nate's concern grew until his pulse rattled against his collarbone like a rock in a pop can. The smell of smoke circled his head like a gray hat.

"The whole south pasture's on fire, boss." Fear laced Beck's comment, though not for himself. Beck was as fearless as they came. Fear for the animals that even now milled and cried in hoarse, frightened chaos.

"Got to move them. Beck, take these men with you." He motioned to the other three cowboys. "The fire's moving north. Start herding the biggest groups west toward the lake. Even if the fire moves that direction, the lake will stop it."

He didn't need to say the rest. The houses and barns were north, and Whitney's ranch was east. Any direction but west was a real danger.

Beck and the boys were gone before he finished talking. He rode close to the fire as sirens wailed through the smoke. The Calypso firefighters would do their best, but they were volunteers on a short budget, and with only one pumper truck. It was up to the men of the Triple C to make up the difference.

The buckskin beneath him fidgeted. Nate patted the dependable animal. "Easy, Unc."

He dismounted and led the buckskin as close to the fire as possible. Thick, choking smoke stopped his progress long before the flames did.

Ace shouted orders, and men raced along the fire line

slapping embers with saddle blankets they'd soaked in a nearby pond.

"I'm going to the house for the crop sprayer," Nate shouted.

Ace waved him on and went back to fighting the fire. Already, the men's faces were black with soot. The fire, like a living, breathing dragon, grew brighter and bigger.

Though the main house was three miles away, Uncle Buck, a cutting horse and quick as hiccough, made the trip in record time. He, too, felt the tension, the fear that fire generated in both man and animal.

Connie ran to meet him at the barn, her dark face wreathed in worry. She took Uncle Buck's reins.

"You be careful. You be careful." She grabbed Nate around the waist and hugged him hard, a spate of Spanish prayers flowing from her lips.

Nothing terrified Connie more than fire. As a child in Mexico, she'd lost six siblings and her parents in flames that took her home and everything else she held dear. She'd been the only survivor.

"We'll be all right, Connie." He worked as he spoke, using a double hose to fill the big crop sprayer with five hundred gallons of water. "Gather all the old saddle blankets and gunny sacks we can spare and toss them in the back of my truck. Buckets, rakes, shovels, anything we can fight with. And call Emily."

Another worry. His sister lived alone—her choice—a quarter mile from the big house. The fire could easily move in her direction.

The older woman flew around the barn tossing items into the truck bed with a metallic clatter. "I see the flames from the kitchen. I say to Ace, 'Fire. Ace, there is fire.' But I can't see where."

Nate paused long enough to smile at her. "You're the hero of the hour, Connie. Far south pasture."

She handed him a box of leather gloves and another of paper dusk masks they used when handling grain or working large herds in the Oklahoma heat and dust. "Take these."

He tossed the items onto the seat of his truck and leaped inside. He put the truck in reverse, backed to the spray rig, then got out again. Connie rushed to help hitch the trailer and, in minutes, Nate was ready to roll.

"It may be a long night." Then more grimly, "Watch the house and barns, call every hand and neighbor we know. And keep praying."

WHITNEY SMELLED smoke as she mucked out Clive's stall. The feisty stallion was on parole in the fenced barn lot where she could keep an eye on him, and the twins were in the empty stall next to this one. Every few minutes, she peeked over the top to see them happily playing on the bed of clean straw. A stall wasn't exactly the best play room, but it was the cleanest, safest solution she could think of out here in a barn that demanded her attention.

Confident the twins were safe, she stepped into the open lot and sniffed the air as she turned in a slow circle, searching for the source of smoke.

She'd turned a half moon to the right when she spotted the gray cloud boiling taller and wider by the second. Every piece of grass and dirt beyond her ranch belonged to the

Triple C. While the thought settled, heavy as lead, the sirens grew louder until a single fire truck sped past her house.

"The south pasture." Her pulse clattered in fear.

Nate's south pasture must be on fire, and he was working out there today. He'd been on his way when he'd left her ranch.

A slow, sinking dread drifted over her. Even a city girl knew grass fires in this dry weather were dangerous. Fire danger had been high since before her arrival. She'd seen the signs all over town and heard the warnings on the radio. A burn ban was in effect.

In seconds, two pickup trucks raced past spewing dust. Neighbors helping neighbors.

She was tempted to phone Nate but knew he would be too busy battling fire to talk. Instead, she found the Triple C number and tapped it.

Connie answered, breathless and worried.

"It's Whitney. I see the smoke. Is everyone okay?"

"So far, but *mija*, I worry. The grass is tall and so very dry. Even the woods are dry. And the wind—"

"I know. I'm worried too. Does Emily know?" She cast a glimpse at the darkening sky. Darkening, not from the late hour, but from smoke obliterating the sun.

"She is on her way here."

"I want to help. What can I do?"

"Come to the ranch. We will cook, we will pray, and we will make ready for a long night."

As soon as she rang off, Whitney took the girls inside the house for a quick wash-up, filled their backpack, and drove to the Triple C. As she turned under the crossbars emblazoned with three interconnected horse shoes and traveled the half-mile back to the main house, she was reminded of the enormity of the property. She'd barely paid attention before, but miles of fence and yellowed grass extended as far as her eyes could see. Groves of trees and bodies of waters dotted the landscape grazed by large herds of black cattle. Here and there in the distance she spotted a pond or a house and a splash of timber.

The main house, when she reached it, was an older, sprawling two-story with dormers. A flat concrete porch, held up by native and rock pillars, ran the home's length. Nestled behind two majestic trees, the rock house was surrounded by beds of bright, fall flowers, and big pots of yellow and orange mums stood sentry by the front door, a testament to Connie's love of flowers and color.

The front door opened before she could ring the bell. Emily, black eyebrows wrinkled in worry, welcomed her inside.

"Any update?" Whitney shifted the backpack to the foyer floor and loosened her death grip on the twins' hands.

"The fire is bad and spreading fast. We need to plow a fire break around the house and each of the barns. Just in case."

In case the fire came this far. In case this gorgeous home and ranch went up in flames. Whitney suppressed a frightened shudder. This was no time for hysterics.

Connie appeared from the adjacent room, hands twisting in her apron, her normally dark skin ashen. "Gilbert came to get fresh water. He is worried. Already the men are exhausted."

"Is Nate okay?" Whitney badly wanted to follow the smoke and make sure Nate was safe. But she'd take her cues from the women. They understood the situation far better than she.

Emily and Connie exchanged not so subtle looks. She didn't care. She was worried about her ranch hand. And her friend.

"Everyone is safe for now."

For now sounded ominous. Goosebumps rose on Whitney's arms. "How can I help?"

"Can you drive a tractor?" Emily shoved her jeans into the tops of cowboy boots. She didn't look a thing like the professional social worker Whitney had first met.

"I'm a fast learner." She might be a city girl but, she was no wimp. Scared, unsure, yes. Wimp, no. "There's a tractor on my ranch. I need to learn."

"Good. Connie's needed here. She mans the phones and keeps the men apprized of updates from the county and each other. I'll show you what you need to know."

"I will watch the little ones." Connie squatted beside the twins for a double hug. The girls must have remembered the ice cream, because they stuck to the Mexican woman like magnets. Connie gazed up with wide, dark eyes.

"Fire frightens me, *mija*. I know God says to have no fear, but my boys are out there...my *familia*." Her voice trailed away. "I cannot lose them, too."

Pity touched Whitney's heart. Connie had lost someone to fire. No wonder she was afraid.

She squeezed the older woman's forearm. With more confidence than she felt, she said, "Don't worry. We'll do everything we can, and we'll pray."

Connie gave a hard nod, chin set. "The cowboys like my chili, and I have a big, big pot. I will cook and make coffee and iced tea. Yes, we will be ready. God will protect them."

"You sure you don't mind watching the twins while I help Emily?"

Connie waved her off. "It will be a pleasure. A-how you say?-distraction. Go now. Do what you can."

The dear little woman, with the twins toddling along on either side, left Emily and Whitney alone in the foyer.

"Ready?" Emily asked.

Ready as she'd ever be. "Let's go."

As they crossed the back yard to the huge building Emily termed the tractor shed, they both cast anxious glances toward the south.

Black smoke billowed across a glowing sky. "That's nasty looking."

"Fire out here is scary business. Three years ago, we lost two firefighters in a brush fire. And I—" Emily's lips tightened. She shook her head. "Bad thoughts. Sorry."

"Are you okay?"

"Connie and I hate fire for similar reasons. We've both lost people we loved."

"I'm sorry." Whitney wanted to ask for details, but right now, they had a task to do. "Are you sure you can teach this city slicker how to drive a tractor?"

They reached the shed, and Emily twirled the dial on a padlock and elevated the overhead door. Inside were parked four tractors and several large farm implements Whitney didn't recognize. Emily let the way to the smaller of the tractors.

"It will take both of us to attach the plows. Then I'll show you the essentials."

Working together, they connected the required implements, and Whitney listened intently to a crash-course in tractor gears.

"I'll drive us out, engage the plow and get you started. Then you take the wheel and plow around the hay barns while I plow around the house and horse barn. There are other barns farther out. I'll check with Ace to see if those are in danger. Got your cell with you?"

Whitney patted her pocket, thankful the pushy cowboy had insisted she take the device. "And your number is already programmed in."

In far less time than she would like, Whitney was alone for the first time in her life inside the cab of a tractor.

Head whirling with information and not a little fear that she might drive the tractor over a cow or hit a tree, Whitney slowly edged the enormous machine forward.

There were two shifters and, thankfully, Emily had engaged both and told her to leave them be. She'd instructed Whitney to drive in a circle around each barn and make sure the plowed area was wide enough to stop the fire. Thirty feet at least. She could do that.

Praying for Nate and the other firefighters, for the fire to go out, and for herself to do this right, she guided the big machine around the first barn and then the second. An acre away, she saw a spot of bright orange that was Emily's tractor circling the big house. Farther still, she saw the smoke. She hoped it was her imagination, but the fire seemed to be moving closer.

After what felt like an eternity but was probably less than thirty minutes of circling in the giant machine, Emily directed her to park the tractor. Whitney shut down and hopped out, feeling ridiculously accomplished. "I can't believe I just did that."

Emily offered a smile and a high five. "Hopefully, that's the last for the night. Ace said to leave the other barns."

"The fire must not be close."

"Or too close for our safety."

Whitney shivered at the ominous reminder, then fell in step with the other woman and hurried back to the house, hoping Connie had news from Nate.

Once inside, Whitney lifted her nose in the air. "Something smells good."

"Connie's five-alarm chili. Burns your tonsils out but tastes incredible."

Emily led the way through the house. The rooms looked comfortable and lived in, the couches and chairs well-worn leather. Over the living room fireplace, a pair of crossed rifles bracketed by spurs bore the Triple C brand. They looked antique.

They passed through the dining room, a long, rectangular space sporting a wall of windows that looked out over the massive back range from whence they'd just come. The Triple C made her ranch seem miniscule.

From somewhere she heard baby chatter. She found the twins playing happily inside the kitchen. They ran to her, and she bent for a hug.

Connie turned from her spot at a counter. "You do it? You drive the tractor?"

A proud grin spread Whitney's lips. "Emily's a good teacher."

"My Emily. She is smart. You, I think, are smart too."

Emily kissed Connie's check. "She is. She caught on right away. If the fire comes close, the house and nearest outbuildings should be safe."

"Unless the fire is too wild or the wind too high."

"Don't borrow trouble, Connie."

Connie waved expressive hands. "I know. I know. My faith is weak tonight for some reason."

"For good reason."

"You too, *mija.*"The older woman patted Emily's cheeks. "You are too warm. I will get some iced tea for you."

"I'll get it."

"Were the babies good, Connie?" Whitney took the glass Emily passed to her from an overhead cabinet and filled it with iced tea.

"*Muy bueno.* So good, I would not mind having them live in this house. I would be a *bueno abuela*, a grandmamma."

Whitney caught Emily's glance. The social worker grinned. "She's an unapologetic matchmaker, Whitney. You might as well marry one of my brothers and get it over with."

Whitney nearly choked on her tea. "After the fiasco with the twins' father, I'm out of the romance market for good."

Emily offered a fist bump. "You and me both, sister. Jessica—that's my best friend. You met at her church. She and her husband Scott are expecting their first baby, and she keeps making noises about me getting married again."

"Again?"

"I'm a widow."

"*Sí.* A widow for almost six years. I try to find her a man, but she is never happy."

"I *am* happy, Connie, with my job, my house, my friends, and my church. I don't need another husband."

Connie sniffed. "But no babies. How I gonna be *abuela* if none of you stubborn Caldwells get married?" She waved a long butcher knife toward Whitney. "But you like our Nate, and he likes you. I am his heart mama. I know. Yes?"

Emily laughed out loud.

Connie could say more in one breath than her adopted son said all day.

Heat, hot as the grass fire, rose in Whitney's cheeks. "Nate has been a real lifesaver."

"His wife was no good, you know, but it is not my place to say." Connie frowned and chopped a stack of chili peppers with enough vehemence to send a clear message. Don't mess with Connie's kids.

Whitney stepped to the stove and stirred the frying meat. The smell was spicy and mouth-watering. "I've wondered."

Emily took a large block of cheese from the refrigerator. "Alicia was a spoiled brat who ran Nate in circles."

"You didn't like her."

Emily shrugged. "We all tried, but she thought we were country bumpkins, and she was some kind of princess. The fact that Nate treated her like one made things worse."

"Not that it's my business, but he seems like such a nice, solid guy."

"Yes, *exactamente*." Connie pointed the huge butcher knife again. "But now, *you* are here."

"We're only neighbors, Connie. He's helping me out. That's all." That's all it could be. She needed his help too much to mess up their relationship with romance.

Connie waved away her denial as if it didn't count while Emily grated cheese into a huge bowl. The twins toddled around the kitchen banging on plastic bowls and lids and singing indecipherable songs. Once in a while, one of them stopped in front of Connie and jabbered something. The Mexican woman replied in Spanish and offered them a grape.

After one such episode, Connie wiped her hands on the apron and went to the window.

"How's it look?" Whitney asked.

"Bad."

Whitney's pulse jumped. She gave the meat a quick stir before going to the window to see for herself. Connie hadn't exaggerated. The smoke grew thicker and the darkening sky glowed with an eerie brightness.

Emily joined her. A quick intake of breath confirmed her fears. This was bad. Very bad.

"I wish someone would let us know what's happening," Whitney said. She hoped Nate and the others were safe. She wished he'd come to the house. She wished he wasn't out there at all.

Connie chopped a pile of onions and tossed them into the meat. Whitney returned to her station at the stove.

"Maybe I should drive down and check on them, "Emily said. "Take fresh water or tea. They may need our help out there."

Connie shook her head. "You phoned Ace, no? He said stay put. It's too dangerous."

"It's getting late." Emily continued to stare out the window. "They must be starved. Surely, they'll come soon."

"If they can." Connie's tone was ominous as the smell of smoke seeped into the house.

Time seemed to drag. With each passing moment, Whitney grew more antsy. She thought about phoning Nate, but what if he was close to the flames and a call put him in jeopardy? Besides, what would she say? "I like you too much, and I'm scared something might happen to you?"

No, better to take her cues from the Caldwell women, who kept busy with food preparations, radio reports, and updates from the country sheriff and emergency management. Twice, Ace phoned Emily, but he never mentioned Nate.

Connie continually paced to the window to mutter in Spanish. Prayers, Whitney thought, and she was saying plenty of her own.

When the evening lengthened, she fed and bathed the twins while Connie formed a makeshift bed between two padded arm chairs. Finally, the girls were asleep.

Whitney was about to head back into the kitchen when she heard a car engine outside. She peeked out the front window, and her heart leaped as the shadowy forms of three men slammed out of the truck and tramped, bedraggled and filthy, into the kitchen.

Nate was not among them.

"Where's Nate?" she blurted. "Is he okay? Is the fire out?"

Three raccoon-eyed males looked at her. Ace, a tall, handsome cowboy with Nate's dark coloring flashed a grin, startling white against the soot-covered face.

Emily shoved a glass of iced tea into his hand, and he took a long drink. The other men stumbled to the counter where Emily passed out more tall, full glasses of sweet iced tea.

"Not yet." Ace said. "Had some reinforcements come in from the Rock Spring's Fire Department so we could take a break. Nate headed over to check on your place."

Nate was okay. *Thank you, Lord.* Right behind the relief came a swell of gratitude. Nate was concerned about her animals, her property.

Then reality struck her. He wouldn't drive to her house without a reason. "Is the fire close to my ranch? Is my house in danger?"

Ace exchanged glances with an older Native American man. Gilbert. "The fire came from that direction. Does Nate know you're here?"

"No." Now she wished she'd followed her instinct and called him.

"That explains it."

Explained what? "Should I text him?"

"Won't do any good. He'll be back soon. He's determined to make sure your animals are safe. Said he has an investment in their well-being."

Oh. So that was it. The animals. Still, she was thankful he'd thought of them.

The cowboy Emily called Beck moved to the stove and moaned his appreciation. "That smells better than Mama's fried chicken right now."

Connie flipped bother hands at him. "Shoo. We will put food on the table while you clean up."

The men traipsed dutifully away, talking in low tones about the cattle and the dangers. While they were gone, she and Connie dished up chili and set out more tea and a red box of saltines next to the bowl of grated cheddar.

At last Nate stomped through the back door. Whitney's pulse jumped as if she'd swallowed a kangaroo. He saw her first thing, and something akin to relief shifted over his features. "You're here."

"Ace said you went to my ranch."

If anything, he looked dirtier and more exhausted than any of the others. How could a smoke- and soot-coated man look so appealing and make her so happy?

"The fire made it to the back fence and stopped."

Her shoulders tensed. She pressed a hand to her heart. "My animals?"

"Restless. Nervous." He shot her a tired grin. "Two of the nannies fainted when I shined a light in their pen."

She returned the grin, so very glad to see him. "That's my nanny girls."

"Where are the twins?" He crossed to the sink and drew a big glass of water, gulping it down in four deep swallows. A few drops sprang free and slid down his chin and neck, slicing a trail through the smoke and dust.

"They're asleep. Connie made a bed out of two chairs in the den."

His head bobbed once, and he released a long breath. "Good. I'm glad you're all here. Stay put until this is over."

He said the words as though he expected her and the twins to be in jeopardy. Had the fire gotten that close to her house?

"I'll dish your chili while you wash up."

He started through to the dining area. "Sounds good. Not much time."

"You're going back out?" Whitney followed him, surprised. "I thought another fire department came to help."

"They're working the fire. Someone has to take care of the stock. The way the fire is spreading, we've got to ride the fences, make sure none are down, and check the first calving heifers. This much excitement could bring on a rash of births." He scrubbed a hand over his face as his brother and the other cowboys returned and scooted past her into the kitchen.

"We'll split up and take sections." Ace scraped a chair away from the giant table and sat, his back straight and tall, the way a seasoned cowboy sits a horse. "Gilbert and Beck will head west. Emily and I will push the calves farther north. Nate, you ride the section closest to Whitney's ranch. Give Scott Donley a call. See if he'll ride over and go with you. None of us should be out there alone tonight."

The brothers traded long stares as if silently communicating something she wasn't allowed to know. The notion that they might be keeping something from her ratcheted her anxiety.

Whitney stepped closer to the table. "I'll ride with Nate."

Connie came to the door, wiping her hands on a dish towel. "And I will babysit *la niñas*."

Nate hadn't taken his eyes off Whitney. "You ride?"

"Don't look so doubtful." She gave a little sniff. "Even city girls learn to ride horses. I rode dressage." At summer camp. When she was fifteen.

"Fancy eastern riding?"

Beck muttered, "Sidesaddle."

The other men guffawed. Whitney laughed too. "When was the last time you watched English riding?"

"Uh, never?" Beck's friendly grin was contagious.

"Figures." She flicked an eyebrow at him for good measure. "I can ride." One of her camp counselors had even said she showed promise.

"She will be good company. She is a smart one." Connie caught Gilbert's attention, clearly urging him to join her point of view.

The Native American's expression softened every time he looked at Connie, so it was no surprise when he said, "Let her go, Nate."

One of the other men cleared his throat. Nate glared at him.

"We need all hands on deck." Ace spooned in a huge bite of chili. "Scott has property of his own to protect and a pregnant wife. He's not a sure thing."

"If she's up for it, take her along." Gilbert reached for the cracker box. "We got plenty of good horses."

"She's up for it." Emily patted Whitney's back. "She drove the John Deere and plowed around two of the barns. This girl can do anything."

Nate's eyes found hers. "You did?"

Pride flashed through Whitney. "Emily's a good teacher."

"Maybe, but you did what had to be done." Emily shot a challenge toward Nate. "Which means she can ride pasture with you."

A dozen emotions flickered over Nate's fire-darkened face.

"I'll think about it." He turned on his dusty boot heel and headed down the hall.

"Don't pay him no mind, Whitney." Gilbert winked over a chili bowl piled high with crushed saltines. "He's relieved you and those little ones are safe. He's been fretting like an old lady."

He had? "Exactly how close to my house did the fire come?"

"Can't say for sure, but Triple C land was scorched all the way to the road."

Her eyes widened. "My road?"

A scowling Nate re-entered the room. He'd washed away the worst of the grime and combed his hair. "Don't scare her, Gilbert."

"Scare me? About what?"

Nate settled at the table next to the blond, whiskered Beck. Whitney slid a thick bowl filled with chili in front of him. Between the four men, the dining room smelled like a barbecue pit.

Whitney didn't take their silence as a good sign. "Is something wrong that I don't know about?"

The cowboys shoveled food into their faces for a few bites while she fumed and wondered what was going on.

"Might as well tell her, Nate." Gilbert pointed a spoon at the scowling cowboy. "She'll find out sooner or later."

Whitney slapped both palms onto the table top. Beck jumped. "You guys are starting to make me mad. Find out what?"

Tension, like tightly strung barbed wire, radiated across the room and landed right between Whitney's shoulder blades.

Finally, Nate huffed out an aggravated noise and said, "Looks like the fire started near your place."

"My place? But how?"

All four men locked eyes on her while Connie stood near the table, hands twisting in her apron.

Nate's answer was grim. "That's what we'd all like to know."

7

F or Whitney, Nate saddled Spark, a blood bay mare with the temperament of a veteran who knew her job and didn't mess around. Regardless of riding ability, which he seriously questioned, Whitney would be safe on Spark. At least she was willing to try. And he couldn't help but be impressed that she'd plowed the fire-break. The woman had spunk.

He'd nearly had a heart attack when he'd seen how close the fire was to her back fence. All kinds of crazy scenarios raced through his head. She'd accidentally set fire to the house. The hay he'd helped her move into the barn three days ago had combusted. She and the twins were trapped, gasping for air.

But none of that had happened. She'd been securely at the Triple C with Emily and Connie. And now he was taking her out into the inferno.

Wasn't he the mighty protector?

Giving the cinch one more tug to insure Spark wasn't holding her breath, he stepped back.

Whitney stood at the mare's head, stroking the gentle animal under the chin. "She's beautiful."

"Twice as big as those toys of yours."

"I don't think Sally intended her babies to be ridden."

He huffed. "Only by munchkins and leprechauns."

Whitney laughed, a tinkly sound that reminded him of wind chimes.

"You don't have to do this. You'll be safer in the house."

Her hand paused on the bridle. "I'm not afraid."

He was, but not of the fire. It was the crazy thoughts he was having. He wanted her beside him, with him, close.

The smoke must have addled his brain. "We may have a long night."

"I have two babies. Long nights I can handle."

He supposed she could. He made a stirrup with his hands. "Mount up."

She looked at him for one long moment before sticking her foot into his cradled hands. He boosted her up and adjusted the stirrups to a perfect fit. And if his fingers lingered on her foot, he tried to pretend the touch was accidental.

With Uncle Buck geared up and eager to work, Nate swung into the saddle. Together, Nate and Whitney rode out into the smoky night. From the corner of his eye, he watched her ride. She sat the saddle with effortless form, her hands light on the reins. A speck of Nate's tension seeped away. Maybe she actually did know a little something about horses. And maybe, just maybe, he could keep her safe.

"Don't we need a flashlight?" Whitney's question came as the house lights faded behind them and the swirling smoke turned them to silhouettes.

"You've got glow sticks in the saddle bag if you need them. Spark doesn't. Horses have good night vision."

"I didn't know that." She turned toward him in the saddle, close enough to touch. "It's beautiful out here at night. If not for the fire..."

Nate let his mind finish the sentence, though he had no idea what her thoughts were. If not for the fire, this would be a romantic ride.

In the light of the moon, he could make out Whitney's features, her luminous eyes, the shine of her cinnamon hair as they rode side by side.

"Even the fire has a certain beauty." He scoffed softly. "Not that I want it burning up our winter grazer."

"You said the fire appeared to start on my back pasture. How could that have happened?"

A shiver ran down Nate's arms. Whitney's voice sounded soft and mysterious. The moon, the night, the woman. All were playing havoc with his emotions. He shouldn't have let her come along. Not only for her protection but for his. His neighbor had become a temptation, a constant thought he couldn't shake.

Could he survive that kind of hurt again?

"We'll ride out there tomorrow and take a closer look. Maybe a careless smoker or a spark from a car engine started the blaze." Neither idea seemed practical, given that her land adjoined his on the inside, not at the road. "We sure haven't had any lightning in a while."

"I wish it would rain."

"You and me both." He motioned with his gloved hand. "Look down."

In the moonlight, the scorched land cast a dark shadow.

The smell, acrid and sooty, lifted with the horses' movement.

Whitney sucked in a quick breath. "The fire was *this* close?"

Grimly, he nodded. "We beat it back, but I was starting to worry. Good thing you and Emily plowed that firebreak."

She fell silent, and he knew she was wondering about her own house. He wouldn't tell her. None of the others would either. But if not for a very fortunate wind switch, the fire would have burned her out.

WHITNEY'S SADDLE creaked as she shifted position, seeking comfort and wondering at her temerity. She hadn't been on a horse in years and already her back and legs twinged from the effort to look like she knew what she was doing. If she was going to be a rancher, she had to learn to ride well. Not that this was the time or the place, but she'd jumped at the chance to be with Nate. The impulsive action was the kind of the thing the old, reckless Whitney would have done... and it scared her.

They rode for a while without conversation, eyes scanning the vast pasture. Whitney remained acutely aware of the cowboy at her side, of how much she'd grown to like him in such a short time. It was as though all her long-dead nerve endings came alive when he walked into a room. Her anxiety seeped away. Everything would be all right because Nate was there.

Leather groaned as the cowboy on her mind leaned over the saddle horn and squinted into the night. "I see something up ahead."

He tapped Uncle Buck with his heels and *smooched* at

him. The buckskin responded with a quick leap. Whitney easily urged Spark into a matching quick-step that rattled her bones.

As they approached a milling herd of heifers, Nate slowed the horse and moseyed closer.

"First calving heifers. Better move them up closer to the calving barn in case we have some babies resulting from this scare. We were planning to move them next week anyway."

"How do we do that?"

"The horses do most of the work. Aim Spark toward the back of the herd. Stay slow and easy. Don't get excited, or the cows will spook and scatter. I'll handle the rest."

"Right." As if she understood what he was talking about.

She followed the cowboy's lead, letting the little mare dip and turn and move the cattle in a slow waltz. Occasionally, one cow bawled and another answered as they ambled forward, unhurried and unstressed, dark shadows in the moonlight. The movement was smooth clockwork, an ancient rhythm of man, horse, and cattle that everyone seemed to understand and take for granted except her.

Nate's voice was soft and as mysterious as the night sky. "Sometimes out like this at night, I think about the old west. What it would have been like to sleep under the stars for days. The dangers and adventures. No towns for miles. Only cows and coyotes for company."

"Lonely. Scary."

He laughed softly. "Maybe I was born a century or two too late. It sounds romantic to me." He stopped and cleared his throat. "Not that kind of romantic."

"I knew what you meant." Letting Spark do all the work of moving cattle, she focused on the man. The moonlight gilded him, reflecting off the pearl shirt buttons in shiny white. He was a silhouette that glowed in the dark, a hat-shaped photograph of days gone by. "Did you always want to be a rancher?"

Nate's hat pointed toward the cattle, attuned to their every motion. "I grew up here and, after I left, I always knew I'd return sooner or later. Preferably later."

His answer surprised her a little. He seemed to be part of the land, as if he'd always been here. "What happened?"

"My dad died. Heart attack. I talked to him on the phone the night before, and he sounded fine."

She heard the pain behind his words. "Nate, I'm so sorry."

"Yeah. Bad deal. But that last conversation is a real good memory. I'm thankful God gave us that. Dad nagged me a little about getting good grades. Told me to hurry up and get my license so I could come home and fill the gap left by Doc Franklin."

She rotated toward him. "License for what?"

"I was in my second year of vet school." Hands light on the reins, he repositioned the gelding to head off a wandering heifer. Though the animal hadn't escaped the herd, Nate had intuitively guessed her intent.

"I can see you as a vet. You have a way with the animals." She smiled into the darkness. "Even the mini ones you think of as toys."

"Animals and I understand each other, I guess." There was a smile in his voice. "Even the toy ones."

"So you dropped out of vet school when your dad died?" A shame. A crying shame. He would be a terrific animal doctor. He already was in many ways.

"Had to. Ace was going through some stuff and had problems of his own. I was needed here. The Triple C is our legacy. Too many big ranches are disappearing because family members lose interest. I didn't want that to happen. Dad worked too hard to make the ranch what it is, to give us kids an inheritance."

"What about your other brother and sister?"

"Neither of them love the land or the animals the way Ace and I do. Wyatt's full time military. And Emily...well, Emily loves the ranch, but her heart is in her work with kids. I'm all about animals. She's all about kids."

"Sad she didn't have any of her own. She told me a little about her late husband."

"We keep hoping she'll find a nice guy and remarry, have a couple of babies." His teeth flashed in the darkness. "Connie most of all, but Emily's had her heart broken a couple of times, and when Dennis died, a wall went up."

"Grief can do that."

"Yeah. It sure can."

Whitney heard something in his tone and wondered if he spoke of himself. Divorce was a kind of death. Did he still grief for his ex-wife?

None of Whitney's business, so she didn't ask. "Do you ever wish you hadn't left vet school?"

He didn't answer for a minute or two while the cattle shuffled and *merred* and a distant pump jack beat rhythm for an oil company.

"God blessed me with this ranch, and I get to work with animals every day. Calypso has no vet, and since I know a thing or two, I help out where I can." He slowed Uncle Buck with a gentle tug. "How can I complain about what I don't have when I have so much and lots of folks have so little?"

"No regrets, then?"

He chuckled softly. "Plenty of those, but not about

ranching or vet school. I'm content. What about you? What did you want to do other than watch goats faint and try to keep Clive from escaping?"

She heard the teasing in his words and kept her answer light. "What more could a girl want?"

But her thoughts flashed back to the girl she'd wanted to be. Like most teenagers, she'd had dreams. When an older guy came along and captivated her immature heart with promises of love and excitement, she'd thought he was the fulfillment of those dreams. She'd run away with him. In the process, she'd broken her parents' hearts, and she hadn't even cared. Life was fun, exciting, and when Ben hadn't worked out, Elliot waited in the wings.

She'd learned the hard way that every action has consequences.

How did she tell a solid man like Nate, a man who always seemed to do the right thing, about a life that had gone off the tracks?

Nate eased his horse closer to hers. "Did I bring up a bad subject? You got really quiet."

"No, no." Except he had. She gave a little laugh. "When I was in high school, I wanted to be a teacher, but then I discovered boys." And a lot of other things that weren't good for her.

"And got sidetracked?"

"You could say that." She bit down on her lip and stared into the smoke-scented night.

"Want to talk about it?"

Did she? And let him know what a loser she was?

Maybe she should. Given the emotions he stirred, the best thing she could do was scare him off. "I left home at seventeen. Ran away."

"That's really young. Bad home life?" His voice was soft, understanding, and invited confidence.

"I wish I could say it was, but no. Maybe mine were not the most involved parents and certainly not strong disciplinarians, but I was the problem. Rebellious, foolish. Of course I didn't think so at the time. I met an older guy. I was madly in love. Mostly with myself."

"Ah, now, lots of kids go through a rough patch. You couldn't have been that bad."

"I was." She swallowed down the thick knot of regret. "So bad that my parents eventually cut me off for good. They were done."

"Harsh."

"Not really. They never heard from me unless I wanted money or was in trouble. They finally stopped taking my calls."

"At all? When was this? Before or after the twins?"

"They knew I was pregnant because I asked them for money to leave Elliott. That was the last time we spoke."

"Elliott? The twins' father?"

Whitney nodded, hair brushing the tops of her shoulders. "We'd been together for a couple of years, so when I got pregnant, I pushed him to marry me. After that, everything went downhill. He hated the idea of marriage. Told me to get rid of the problem, as he called the babies, but I couldn't do that. Then I gave my life to Christ and started to change, and things really got bad. My old ways felt tawdry, wrong. We fought so much, I was scared. I wanted to leave, but I was totally dependent on Elliott for support. No education. No skills. And we had babies coming. Or rather I did. He'd made it clear, he wanted no part of parenting."

"Having the twins was the last straw?"

"Yes." She shook her head sadly, remembering the hurt and shock of having nowhere to go. "Before I got home from the hospital, he'd changed the locks on the house and left my clothes in trash bags on the sidewalk."

Whitney pressed a hand to her lips. What had come over her? She'd never told that story to anyone. Why had she told Nate, of all people? He was a Christian who'd probably never done a bad thing in his life.

She sneaked a peek in his direction. Was he disgusted? Revolted? And who could blame him if he was? She was disgusted with herself.

He moved the horse closer until his leg brushed hers.

"Hey. I'm sorry."

So was she. "My own fault."

"We all mess up. That's why we need Jesus." Tone gentle, he gave her knee a comforting squeeze.

"He sure had a lot to forgive when He got me. I don't know where I would be today if I hadn't found Him."

She could still remember how she felt, three months pregnant, stumbling into a Christian pregnancy center after a major fight with Elliot, desperate and scared. That was where she'd found the greatest source of help in the universe—a relationship with the Savior.

"Now you can work on forgiving yourself."

"Is that even possible?"

He was quiet for a second. When he spoke, his soft reply barely reached her ears. "I sure hope so."

Then he turned Uncle Buck with a click of his tongue and circled until his back was to her.

Had she revealed too much and lost his respect?

Not that she deserved anyone's respect, certainly not a salt-of-the-earth man like Nate Caldwell.

"Got a straggler." He pointed with his chin.

A straggling cow. Not a rejection of her.

Breathing a relieved sigh, Whitney squinted to make out the dark bovine shape in the distance. "She's not moving at all."

"We're almost to the gate. We'll haze these through and come back for her." He edged around the herd and rode ahead to open the gate, leaving Whitney to wonder. What was he thinking now that he knew her ugly history? Was he sorry he'd befriended her? This was supposed to have been her fresh start, her break from the past. And now he knew the truth of it.

She shouldn't have told him.

Why did his opinion matter so much anyway?

With a low groan, Whitney lifted her face toward the sky and wished for the millionth time that she could go back in time and start her life over. But she couldn't, and God had given her this opportunity to move forward. Time to stop fretting and get busy.

With no encouragement from her rider, Spark nosed the herd forward. Once the leaders started through the opening, the rest followed easily.

Metal clanked as Nate shut the gate, and in minutes they'd returned to the lagging heifer. By now, the animal was on the ground, big eyes gleaming in the moonlit.

Nate slid from his horse and knelt on the dry grass next to the heifer.

"Is she sick?"

Cowboy hands stroked the animal, feeling her massive belly. "In labor. I'll need the flashlight out of my saddlebag."

"I'll get it." Slowly, painfully, Whitney dismounted and walked stiffly to the buckskin. Every muscle in her legs and back ached. She didn't even want to think about how she'd feel tomorrow.

Spark turned her head to watch the humans but made no attempt to wander away. Like Nate's gelding, the mare wasn't tethered and yet she waited patiently for her rider. The horses had done this before.

"How do we help?" Whitney asked.

"I'd like to get her up and move her to the barn." Nate glanced in the direction of the fire. "I don't see flames anymore. Hopefully, the men have it under control, but I don't like to take any chances. If she's down calving and fire sweeps through here—"

He didn't have to complete the gruesome thought. Whitney got the idea.

"Do you think the blaze is out?"

"Hard to tell from this far away." He took the flashlight from Whitney and shined it on the heifer. Gently, he pushed at the animal's hips. "Come on, Bee, get up."

"Bee?" Gingerly, Whitney squatted beside him, fighting not to groan at her sore thigh muscles.

"Her tag number. B56."

"Bingo!" Whitney stifled a giggle. She was getting giddy with fatigue.

Nate glanced up with a tired smile. "She's too far along to get to the barn."

"What do we do?"

"Stay with her. Make sure nature does the right thing." He motioned toward Spark. The mare stood at Whitney's back, snuffling her shoulder. "Can you find your way to the house?"

"I think so. Why?"

"You should go. I'll stay."

She shook her head. "No."

He pushed up from the ground and ambled toward his horse, two shadowy hulks in perfect tune. "I'll likely toss a blanket on the ground. Could be a long night. You'll be more comfortable at the house."

"I want to stay." She backed against the mare, feeling the solid heat of horseflesh. "I need to learn these things, Nate. All my animals are pregnant, and you may not be around when one of them gives birth."

The thought struck pure terror in her soul. Nate certainly did not need her help, but the opportunity to learn was real.

She didn't examine the other reason.

He studied her in the dim light before his head bobbed once. "Okay, then. If you're sure. Good a time as any to learn."

She let out a breath, aware she'd expected him to send her away, and even more aware that she wanted to be with him. "I am. Thank you."

His head tilted. "For?"

She circled a hand in the air. "Everything. For being so nice. For being..." Her voice trailed away as Nate stepped closer.

"For being what?" His breath was warm on her cheek, his brawny body blocking the chill in the smoky wind.

Warm horse behind, warm man in front, she was cocooned and comfortable. Safe. Secure. Two things she hadn't been in years.

"For being you."

He laughed softly. "Yeah, I'm really something."

Didn't this incredible man know his value? Or had his

walk-away spouse worked a number on this cowboy's self-esteem?

Empathizing, Whitney touched his chest with the tips of her fingers. "Yes. You are. You said God blessed you with this ranch. Well, he blessed me with mine, too, and with you to teach me the things I have to know to get through this next year. I don't take that lightly. You'll never know how very much your generosity means."

His gloved hand captured her fingers, but when she thought he'd push her away, he simply held on. Not pushing away, not pulling forward.

The air shifted. Each seemed to ponder the other, taking stock, wondering.

Behind her, the mare shuffled, nudging at her back. Whitney rocked forward. Nate caught her, and suddenly, they were heart to heart. She laughed, self-conscious, but didn't step away. Neither did Nate.

So she was not a bit surprised when he lowered his head and brushed his lips across hers.

She was, however, surprised at the rocket of emotion exploding in her damaged heart.

8

N ate hunkered behind the heifer, aware he'd have to assist the birth if the baby didn't deliver in the next few minutes. The first-time mama was fast approaching exhaustion. When she reached that point, she'd give up, and the valuable calf would die.

He glanced at Whitney, asleep a few feet away on the blanket he carried in his saddle bag.

He'd finally convinced her to rest for a while when it became apparent that the birth would take some time. She'd smoothed out the blanket on one condition—he wake her as soon as the calf appeared. In two minutes, she'd been fast asleep. The calf's hooves had appeared thirty minutes ago, but he was reluctant to disturb his sleeping neighbor.

Truth was, the kiss had rattled him. He didn't know why he'd kissed her. He hadn't wanted to kiss a woman in a long time. Hadn't wanted to care about a woman ever again. Not in that way. But when she'd told him that awful story about her ex-boyfriend's abandonment, he'd wanted to hit something. Preferably her ex. But Whitney hadn't asked for his sympathy. She'd taken responsibility for her mistakes, had admitted she'd made bad choices. Not many people did that anymore.

Alicia certainly hadn't.

He pulled a hand over his face, considering his unlikely feelings for his neighbor. His friend. Did he want her to be more? Would she want that too?

He didn't know, but he did know this much. Whitney plucked a chord in him that had gone silent months before Alicia left. During that time, his wife had chipped away at his love on a daily basis until he'd felt nothing at all. Then, tonight when he'd kissed Whitney, only a faint brush of lips, his music played again. Heart music.

He shook his head hard to toss out the poetic thoughts. He was tired. Crazy thoughts ran through a man this time of night, alone in the darkness with stars winking at him and the moon smiling, and with a beautiful woman sleeping nearby.

He rose and walked the few steps to where Whitney slept. He crouched beside her. She lay curled on her side, arms huddled against her body, her long hair fanned out behind her. She was probably cold. He should have covered her, but then, according to Alicia, he was lousy at understanding a woman's needs.

"Whitney." Not wanting to startle her, he whispered first and then touched her shoulder.

Her eyes popped open. "Is it time?"

His lips curved. "You wake up fast."

"I'm a mother." She sat up, shoving hair away from her face. He itched to do that for her, to smooth the long, silky hair and snuggle her close, to warm her with his body.

Catching his train of thought, he stood and reached

down for her. Soft hand in his, he pulled her to her feet. She took a moment to stretch. He knew better than to watch those lithe movements of the female form, especially now when his head was messed up with thoughts of her. He went back to the heifer. Behind him, Whitney's back popped, and he smiled again.

"Ground isn't the softest bed," he said.

"I don't mind. I'm grateful for the rest."

There she went again. City girl had some steel in her spine.

"Ready for a lesson I hope you won't have to use? We're going to have to help the heifer."

"The baby won't come on its own?"

"No. And the mama is getting tired."

"Poor thing." Whitney smoothed a hand down the cow's back. "Labor and delivery isn't for sissies."

"Neither is pulling a calf." He slid a glance at her. "You ready for this?"

Her chin came up. "Ready as I'll ever be."

A tired smile lifted Nate's lips. City girl or not, a man had to admire a woman with grit.

A FEW HOURS BEFORE DAWN, Whitney and Nate returned to the Triple C. Lights still blazed, and they trudged inside to the sound of voices and the smell of bacon.

Connie stood at the stove, a carton of eggs at her elbow, while Ace toasted bread and Gilbert pulled plates from the cabinet.

"Fire's out," Ace said. "You look beat."

"Had to pull a calf. B56."

Whitney almost shouted, "Bingo" again but was too

tired. She giggled instead and received curious looks from the others.To cover her giddiness, she asked the question foremost in her thoughts. "How are the twins?"

"Sleeping like angels. I told these boys to stay in here to eat and talk. Let the babies rest."

"Thank you, Connie."

"You sure you are okay?"

From Connie's sympathetic expression, Whitney figured she looked pathetic, but she refused to play the tired green-horn. "As okay as anyone else."

Truth was, Whitney's whole body ached, but she hadn't felt this energized in months. She was running on adren-aline for three good reasons. The calf. The man. The kiss.

"At daylight," Ace said, "we'll drive around the burned areas and see what's lost. Did you get the fall heifers moved?"

Nate removed his hat to run a hand through his hair, a weary motion. "To the back lot. All safe. Even the new mama and her baby bull."

"Is there anything else I can do to help before I go home?" Whitney asked.

"Eat." Gilbert poked a plate at her. "We feed our hands."

"She's a good one." Nate caught her gaze and held on. "Not a whimper of complaint, and she helped deliver that calf like a pro."

They both knew she hadn't done much, but Whitney was struck by how much his praise meant. Tonight had been an anomaly. She'd not felt successful at anything in a long, long time.

"You're a good teacher. A good vet, too."

They exchanged secret smiles, the barely-kiss a whisper in the air between them.

Gilbert cleared his throat, and she realized she had yet to accept the plate he offered. Fighting a blush under the surface of her fair skin, she ducked her head and reached for the bacon. Though not before she saw the looks exchanged between Emily and Connie.

AFTER THE LONG NIGHT, the sun rose and Whitney felt as if she'd been hit by a truck, particularly from her mid-back down. Muzzy-headed after less than three hours' sleep, she rose with the babies. Both girls were full of energy and well rested. Naturally.

Nate, who had to be more exhausted than she, texted her at seven and met her at the barn fifteen minutes later. He looked as tired as she felt. Tired but good. Solid. Dear. And if her heart beat a little fast when he glanced her way, she pretended otherwise.

Not that she mentioned any of this to him.

They talked of the fire, the animals, the men who'd come to help, and the way Calypso pulled together in times of trouble.

What they didn't talk about was the kiss and the feelings brewing under the surface. Which was fine with Whitney. She didn't know what to do with those feelings anyway.

"Over a thousand acres of winter pasture burned," Nate was saying as he unlatched a storage room.

The twins, ever a distraction, ran around the alleyway of the barn, chattering like the rock star hens. They were into everything, and Whitney broke off from work and the conversation to chase Olivia down and remove a glob of debris from a stubbornly clenched fist. The girls, naturally, thought the chase was a delightful game and ran away, giggling.

Meanwhile, Nate worked, doing her job with her animals. Who wouldn't be attracted to a man like that?

The routine was getting easier. It was the non-routine that worried her. "A thousand acres? How do you know for sure?"

Nate hefted a bag of chicken feed and ripped it open with his pocket knife. The dusty smell of meal and grain wafted up. "We drove the burned areas at dawn."

Whitney, reaching for a bucket hanging on a stall door, spun around. "You haven't slept at all? Nate!"

He shrugged off her concern. Muscled shoulders bunched his blue shirt. Another distraction. "I'll nap later."

"Go home. Sleep. I can handle this without your help."

Not that she didn't appreciate and enjoy his company. As far as she was concerned, he could hang out here all day.

A bad sign. A really bad sign.

"You were up too."

"Not all night, and I can nap when the babies do. You should go home." She dipped the bucket into the feed sack. *She* could feed the animals. *He* needed sleep.

"First, I need to talk to you about something." He removed his hat and wallowed his brown hair, a habit she noticed when he was tired or worried, as he appeared to be now.

"What's wrong?" Whitney set the filled bucket on the dirt floor, more concerned about the man than the chickens. Another bad sign. "Did the mama and baby die?"

He stopped her with a hand motion. "Nothing like that."

It must be the kiss. He didn't want her getting crazy ideas. He regretted kissing a woman with an ugly past like hers, a foolish, stupid woman who'd committed more sins in a year than he had in a lifetime. Maybe he was even going to tell her that he couldn't be her teacher anymore. That he didn't want to be associated with a loser like her.

"About that kiss," she blurted before he could say more. "I know it meant nothing. I didn't take it seriously. A kiss between two tired people in the dark. Happens all the time."

Not to her. Not with that kind of sweetness and power. Not ever, but she didn't want to lose him. As her teacher. She didn't expect anything else, even if the kiss had rocked her world.

Nate gave her a long, unreadable stare before taking her arm. "Walk with me."

Her heart rattled in her ears. He was going to kick her to the curb. Tell her to leave him alone. She could take it. She had before. She'd survive. "The twins."

Nate caught Sophia as she raced by. Not to be ignored, Olivia lifted her arms toward him in the universal sign for pick me up. The cowboy lifted both girls into his strong arms. "You need a stroller."

She needed a lot of things. But she didn't expect him or anyone else to take care of her children. Defensive, she reached for her girls. "I can carry them."

He scowled. "I didn't mean that."

Then what had he meant?

NATE BOUNCED the twins as he and Whitney walked side by side through her barn, out the back way, and into the chilly morning. He was worried. No other way to put it. Worried about the woman and kids who were starting to mean a lot more to him than neighbors.

Whitney was holding her own, working hard, and she was a quick learner. That wasn't the problem. The problem was what he and Ace had discovered just outside her fence.

Clive, who now behaved well enough to hang out in the barn lot, ambled from his feed trough to snuffle the humans and beg for treats.

The twins giggled and stretched wiggling fingers toward the animal. Nate tilted them away from the horse's searching mouth. Even if he was gentle, Clive might nip a baby finger thinking it was a carrot. With a *shooshing* sound to let Clive know he meant business, Nate walked to the side of the mini horse and balanced both girls on the hairy back. They got to him, these little girls with their big eyes and sweet giggles. How could any man reject something this precious? And what kind of man was Nate if he didn't keep them safe?

Dark pony tails in flight, Olivia jounced and bounced as if she was riding the mechanical horse at Walmart, her gurgle of laughter sweet in the animal-scented barnyard. Serious Sophia clung to her sister's shoulder with one hand and to Nate with the other.

They were adorable gifts from God, and both had taken to him like horses take to sugar cubes. Not that he was all that sweet, but they sure softened up a spot in the middle of his chest.

Whitney stood on the other side of the short, squatty horse, watchful of her daughters. She was a good mama. Anyone could see that. What he couldn't see was how her boyfriend had dumped her and them so heartlessly. Then again, he'd never understood Alicia either. He was pretty clueless in the human psychology department. Animals he understood. People not so much.

He lifted his face toward the sky, squinting into the glare. The day had dawned gray and cool with a distant hope of rain later. He was feeling a little gray and cool himself, though before he'd come to Whitney's ranch, he'd chalked the gloominess up to fatigue. Now that Whitney had shot him in the chest with her cavalier attitude about last night, about the kiss that made his heart sing, he had no reason to lighten up.

He figured it was for the best. He wasn't any good at the relationship thing, anyway, and he had a weakness for city girls with other plans. He didn't fault Whitney. Unlike his ex-wife, she'd been honest about her intentions.

Still, last night had meant something to him.

Sophia reached for her mama, and Whitney lifted her from the horse's back. Nate swung a protesting, kicking Olivia onto his hip.

"Horse. Horse. Horse." Olivia catapulted her body toward Clive, surprising Nate, who caught her in the nick time to save a crash.

"Whoa, baby girl!" To Whitney he said, "This one's going to be a horse woman like her mama."

Whitney's pale skin pinkened. "About that. I'm a little sore today."

Whitney wasn't a whiner. She probably she felt the ride in every bone of her body. "Haven't ridden in a while?"

She grimaced, a cute, self-mocking look that made him wish for things he shouldn't. "Fifteen years? Summer camp."

"You could have fooled me." He laughed but sobered instantly. She'd fooled him about the other too. The way she'd tiptoed up to meet his kiss. The way her arms strayed to his sides and her fingers kneaded at his shirt, tugging him closer. He'd been sure she'd heard the same heart music.

Fool. That was Nate Caldwell. Easily fooled by women.

Abruptly, he refocused on his mission and walked onward through the lot and out into the pasture land that connected with his property.

Whitney gazed toward the open field. "We're going to see where the fire started?"

She was quick, smart. He knew that about her too. "You need to see it."

Her head swiveled toward him. She looked alarmed. "Why?"

"You'll see." He wouldn't share his suspicions. Not until he had more than gut instinct to go on.

"Down. I walk." Olivia wiggled against him, and he lowered her to the ground.

Sophia, seeing her sister toddling on the yellowed grass, insisted on walking too. The twins stopped to investigate every rock and flower and dead bug along the way. In spite of his somber mood, the babies lifted his spirits. They were the definition of innocence, completely oblivious to their mother's struggles with the ranch, to his worries, to the fire that had come too close to their new home. Babies seemed to take the world at face value and embrace the moment. These two certainly did, but what did he know about babies? Not nearly enough.

The realization made him even gloomier.

"Too bad we can't bottle that unbridled joy," he said.

Whitney paused to remove a beetle from Sophia's hand. This twin easily released the bug. He had a feeling Olivia wouldn't be quite as passive.

"I was thinking the same thing."

They talked as they walked, and he discovered he liked hearing about the twins' milestones and the funny things they did, the differences in their personalities. Already, he could tell them apart by their facial expressions.

Olivia presented him with a crushed yellow wildflower, broom weed and, with a wink he stuck it in his shirt pocket. The little cutie clapped her hands and giggled, a balm to his weariness. The weeds needed to go before they choked out the good grasses, but he reserved that lesson for another time. Like him, Whitney was tired, and she had enough on her mind...with more problems to come.

He ground his back teeth, fretting over what could have happened here last night while Whitney was at the Triple C, what might have happened except for the mercy of God.

By the time they reached the back fence where her land joined his, the twins were in full piggyback mode. Sophia, perched atop his shoulders, patted his hat with both hands and talked nonstop to her sister. Their shouts and giggles and mostly unintelligible words tickled him. He almost felt like a dad.

Nate caught himself up short. Like his sister, he'd always wanted a passel of kids, but life doesn't always pan out the way we hope.

To avoid a fatigue-driven melancholy, Nate corralled the thoughts to focus on the burned landscape spreading out before him. "The fire started here."

Head down, baby hands tangled in her red hair, Whitney held Olivia's legs close to her sides as she studied the five yard swath of scorched grass. Near the T-post just across the fence, in the area where her land met his, was an intensely burned circle.

Whitney's gaze flew to his, a frown between her eyes. "What is that? I don't understand."

"Not sure. Maybe a campfire."

She blinked in surprise. "Why would anyone be camping on the back of your property?"

"You didn't give anyone permission to come in here?" He suspected the answer before she spoke but asked anyway.

Whitney shook her head. The sun shot a different kind of fire through her red hair. He wanted to touch it. To touch her. To reassure her that he would not let anything bad happen. But be it campers or something more sinister, he was concerned that something already had.

"I don't know enough people in Calypso to let anyone camp on my land," she said. "Could one of your cowhands have camped here?"

"Even if they had reason, which they don't, all of them know not to build fires in weather this dry."

He didn't say the rest. That he didn't like the idea that some unknown person had built a fire this close to her land —a fire that had gotten out of control, a fire that would have moved toward her if the wind hadn't shifted. And he worried more than ever about leaving her alone on this ranch with two little ones.

As if feeling the seriousness of the conversation, the twins remained quiet for once. Sophia patted his cheeks every few seconds to remind him she was still on his back. As if he'd forget such precious cargo.

Whitney put a hand to her forehead, more bothered than she seemed to want to let on. "They could have accessed through your land."

"Yes, but they'd have to cross a lot of acres to get here. Coming in from your side makes more sense."

That worried him, too. Unbeknownst to Whitney, someone had trespassed across her property. He couldn't help thinking about L.T., the cowboy he'd tossed out of her barn. He didn't know the man well, but now he wondered. Was L.T. hanging around, waiting for revenge?

Stupid as it sounded, Nate felt responsible for her. Double stupid after she'd blown off that one moment—the kiss—when he'd listened to his emotions instead of his brain. But he couldn't help it. He and Whitney shared similar stories. Exes who strayed, who kicked them in the teeth and hadn't cared when they'd bled. And if that wasn't enough, her hard times were harder than his. She had the twins and not much else, if that old car was an indicator. He had a prosperous ranch, a family, and plenty more. Any cowboy worth his boots would feel sorry for her.

"I don't know what happened here, but you need to be careful. Keep your eyes peeled for any unusual activity."

She flashed wide blue eyes in his direction. Startled eyes. "You think someone set the fire on purpose?"

He'd scared her. Dumb move.

"I didn't say that."

Nor would he bring up the fact that the wind had fortuitously switched directions yesterday, sending the fire toward the Triple C instead of her home.

Like the feelings brewing in his chest, some things were better left unsaid.

9

S everal days passed before Whitney stopped thinking about the mysterious burned spot. She finally decided the fire was purely an accident and wouldn't happen again. As Nate suggested, the trespassers were probably kids who wouldn't think twice about building a campfire regardless of dry grass and burn bans. Then when the fire had gotten out of hand, they'd gotten scared and bolted. End of story. So she put the incident out of her mind and pressed on with learning everything she could from the Triple C cowboy.

The one thing that didn't fade from memory was the midnight ride when Nate had kissed her, the moment when some dead part of her had awakened. If she hadn't dumped her life story on him, maybe he wouldn't have backed away, but she understood why he wanted to be her friendly neighbor and not her man. At least, she was trying to. As much as she wanted to change her past mistakes, she couldn't.

He was right to keep her at arm's length, and even

though she liked him a lot more than she should, friendship was the best choice for both of them. Relationships could be tricky, and she needed his ranching expertise more than she needed romance. God had sent him along to help her, not to be her latest flame, and that was that.

But as weeks passed, Nate spent more and more time at her place, and their friendship grew. And grew. No man had ever listened to her the way Nate did. They could talk for hours and often did. She loved having him in her kitchen scarfing down tiny chicken eggs and gallons of coffee. He seemed to fit there, as if he was the missing ingredient in her life. She loved the easy way he discussed his faith, the sound of his laughter, the way he interacted with the twins.

And every night when she fell into bed exhausted, she prayed a special prayer for this man whose friendship she'd come to treasure.

The day he'd brought the twins a double stroller, she'd almost cried, right before refusing to accept it. He'd gotten adorably huffy and said he'd bought the stroller for the twins, and if *they* didn't like it, he'd take it back. She had no say in the matter.

Because she thought his excuse was cute and clever, she'd given in and thanked him, touched by his generosity. The girls, naturally, thought riding around as a big old cowboy pushed them all over the yard and down the rutted driveway while making truck noises was the coolest thing ever.

So did she. And if she fantasized about someday finding a good dad for Olivia and Sophia, a dad a lot like Nate Caldwell, she kept those thoughts to herself.

On this particular fall morning, when the weather had cooled to crisp, she wrestled a fifty-pound sack of chicken feed out of the back of her car and dragged it, muscles straining, to the self-feeder Nate had showed her how to fill. The twins toddled along behind, having grown accustomed to spending most of their day outdoors with her and the animals.

With a hearty heave, she hoisted the bag up on its edge and filled the tank. A dozen clucking hens raced toward her at the sound, waddling in their funny way as their head feathers swayed in the breeze like hat plumes. Nate was right to laugh. They were silly looking but faithful as the sun in laying eggs every day. Nate called them jelly bean eggs and could eat a dozen. Next spring, and she was determined to be here next spring, he would teach her to set the hens and raise babies to sell for pocket money.

The matter of money, however, was more immediate than next spring, but as Emily and Connie reminded her, she was not alone anymore. With God's help and that of her new friends, she'd figure out ways to generate more income from the ranch. She hoped they were right.

"God didn't bring you here to let you down, *mija*," Connie had said at last week's Bible study. "He has a plan for you, the *niñas*, and this ranch. And His plans are good."

Whitney clung to that belief. God had blessed her with a completely unexpected inheritance. With His help, she not only wouldn't lose the ranch, she would make it thrive. For the first time in her adult life, she was on the right track. She hoped.

She flipped the feeder lid shut and grinned at the funny hens, pecking like mad all around her.

"Come on, girls," she called to the twins. "Let's feed the goats."

Whitney started toward the goat pen. A baby's squeal

turned her around. Her heart leaped into throat. Olivia chased a clucking hen around the pen, but Sophia stood like a wide-eyed statue, frozen in place.

"Sophia! What's wrong?"

The baby opened a hand. "Yucky."

With a relieved laugh, Whitney hustled to her child before Sophia could wipe chicken manure on her clothes. Or worse.

Living and working with animals every day with the twins' in tow worried her, but what else could she do? And hadn't farm women managed on their own for millennia, most of them with far more than two children?

She scooped up the baby, holding her away from her body until they reached the outdoor faucet. The manure smell was strong, but what did she expect? Any girly girl notions she'd brought to Oklahoma had long since vanished. She washed and dried Sophia's hands, using her jeans as a towel.

City girl had come a long way. Nate would be impressed. He'd laugh, too, and probably offer a fist bump. She loved when he did that.

She set a satisfied Sophia on her feet and gave her little back a pat before heading to the barn to get feed for the goats.

The toddlers squealed and raced ahead of her. Lately, their response to everything was an ear-splitting squeal. She watched them, thankful to God that she'd listened to her heart instead of to Elliot. These babies were her very heart-beat. She could not imagine life without them.

Smiling, happy in a way she hadn't been in years, Whitney followed the twins into the barn. The large structure boasted one complete side for storage. The other side housed stalls with a long alleyway between them. Square bales of hay were stacked in the loft for winter feedings. Sally kept a tack room and feed rooms filled with lidded barrels, garden tools, and so much more Nate was teaching her to use.

Hers. All hers. God-willing, she'd turn this ranch into something really special—a home for now and a legacy for her girls' future. Home. Forever. Stable and secure.

She was still working on the last two.

At the feed room, she reached for the door handle but paused. The latch was undone. She frowned, certain she'd secured the door last night. She couldn't afford to lose feed much less allow an animal to get inside and make himself sick.

A creepy feeling prickled the skin on her arms. She looked from side to side. No one. The chickens clucked. The sheep baaed. The billy goat butted his head against the iron gate. Normal, everyday barnyard noises. Nothing else. Nothing amiss.

Pulling the babies close to her side, she shook off the creeps and opened the feed room.

Her stomach fell all the way to the toes of her completely inappropriate snow boots. She couldn't afford work boots.

She also couldn't afford to replace the two bags of corn and sweet feed that were spilled all over the floor of the room.

"How in the world...?" She must have left the door unlocked, and the goats must have gotten in. But how? They were in their pens. "Clive?"

Oh, man, if that dumb horse had escaped and killed

himself on grain, she'd send him to the glue factory. If there was such a thing.

A dark shadow fell across the doorway. "Looks like you have a problem."

Whitney screamed and jumped. Her feet hit the spilled corn, and she slipped, windmilling her arms for a few seconds before collapsing in a cloud of corn dust.

"My deepest apologies. I didn't intend to startle you."

"Mr. Leach." Her pulse banged and thumped louder than the billy goat's incessant head butting. A knot of tension sprang up between her shoulder blades. Lawyer Leach had never paid her a visit. He'd telephoned once to ask how things were going and to make sure she was following the mandates of Sally's will, but this was his first onsite visit.

Now he'd think she was completely incompetent. "The door must have come open and—"

She coughed and grabbed for the twins, who saw the spilled feed as their very own sandbox and gleefully tossed handfuls into the air.

In his brown business suit and yellow striped tie, Lawyer Leach curled his upper lip as if afraid some of the dust would settle on his shiny shoes.

"Does this happen often? Things seem a bit out of control."

"No." Whitney hopped to her feet, brushing corn and grain from her jeans. Some of it trickled into her boots.

She clutched the twins to her side to stop them from resuming their play. Mr. Leach was all business, and she had to show him she was a serious rancher, taking proper care of Sally's farm. "Would you like me to show you around? I promise this has never happened before. I'm not sure why the door was open."

Suddenly, the billy goat's head appeared around the edge of the door. He bleated and started inside, bold as sin. Whitney turned loose of the girls and jumped up, struggling to maintain her footing on the loose feed.

"No, you don't." She caught Billy by the knobby head and pushed him back. How had he gotten through the gate? Had she left that open too?

Lawyer Leach looked on with a troubled expression. "I do hope you aren't in over your head with these animals, Whitney dear. Sally Rogers was a serious rancher who never left feed unsecured. You do understand the ramifications of losing even one of these animals, regardless of your inexperience or neglect."

Neglect? He thought she was neglecting Sally's animals? Her animals? Her children's future?

"I'm so sorry, Mr. Leach. Truly, this hasn't happened before. One of the twins got manure on her hands, and I must have gotten distracted..." Her voice trailed away when his eyebrows edged higher and higher.

Defeated, she wrestled Billy out of the barn and back to his pen. The gate was closed. She frowned, bewildered. Could he have crawled through the rungs? He never had before.

Once the goat was inside and the gate secure, she turned back toward the lawyer, who now picked his way around the pens, avoiding dung and animals even as he inspected them. Apparently, her attorney was not a fan of farm life. And why should he be? He was an attorney looking after her aunt's interests. Interests she did not appear to have under control.

"Things have been going really well." Until now. If he

didn't count the runaway horse and the fainting goats and the fire that started so very close to her fence.

Taking a deep breath and praying to impress with words when she couldn't with actions, Whitney parroted every piece of information Nate had taught her, hoping to prove her competence.

The lawyer rubbed his chin, nodding, eyes narrowed, but making no comment. She was a failure. She could see it in his eyes. If he had to file a report somewhere, he'd give her a big fat F. They'd come and take the farm—whoever *they* was—and give it Ronnie Flood.

"This morning we vaccinated and wormed ten head." She liked how ranchy that sounded, even though her back ached from holding critters in a headlock while Nate squirted pasty stuff down their throats. "We'll get the rest tomorrow."

"We?" Pale eyes settled on her, curious and keen. Mr. Leach had a sharp look about him, but she supposed that was the way of lawyers. Always thinking. Always suspicious. And hadn't she given him plenty to be suspicious about?

"Nate Caldwell, my neighbor. He's teaching me the ropes."

"Caldwell." The man squinted toward the north. "His ranch adjoins Sally's."

She'd begun thinking of the ranch as hers, but she didn't say that. Not yet. A year was a long time.

"You know him?"

The lawyer laughed, though the sound was anything but merry. "Everyone in Calypso County knows the Caldwells. Land hungry. They buy up everything in their path. The rich get richer."

What an odd statement from a lawyer. From her

perspective an attorney who drove a Lincoln and wore fancy suits and shoes was plenty rich. She on the other hand was running a ranch on nothing but a shoestring and hope. "They've been very nice to me."

"He and those brothers of his tried to buy this property after their daddy died. Sally wouldn't sell out."

"I didn't know that." No reason she should. What the Caldwells bought or didn't buy was their business.

Leach scraped the bottom of his shoe on the grass, turned it up and grimaced at the result. Without any further comment, he walked away from the pens and headed for his car, clearly eager to leave. Whitney hustled to keep up, terrified that he'd send her an eviction notice in tomorrow's mail. After all, he was the boss, the lawyer in charge, the executer of Sally's will.

"Would you like to come in for some refreshment?" Maybe a little hospitality could buy her some more time. She racked her brain, hoping she had something besides yogurt and bananas to offer. "Coffee?"

She could always make coffee and eggs, but she doubted her omelets would impress him the way they impressed Nate. Anything to convince him that she and the twins should remain here on the ranch.

He shook his head and slid into the fancy car. "I have an appointment at the office."

Wasn't he going to say anything else? Tell her she was doing okay or that she was out in the cold?

"I'm doing the best I can, Mr. Leach, and I'm working hard to make the ranch a success. Nate says I'm learning fast. Plus," she reminded him, "I still have a long time to prove myself."

There. She'd tossed out her one caveat. The will gave her

a year. Even a lawyer couldn't evict her over spilled feed and a loose goat. Could he?

His sharp eyes narrowed. He slid on a pair of sunglasses and started the car. The engine hummed so quietly, she could barely hear it. Not like her poor battered car with the muffler wired in place.

"One piece of advice, Whitney." Mr. Leach leaned out the lowered window. "You've had some bad luck this morning, and I heard about the fire. Things like that send up red flags. If I were you, I'd keep my eyes on those Caldwells. Just in case."

Then, the darkly tinted window ascended, shutting her out before the lawyer drove away.

Watching the dust and gravel swirl around his shiny clean car, Whitney blinked after him.

In case of what?

10

The young mare lying on the straw inside Ben Stalling's horse barn struggled to a stand. She was wobbly and exhausted but beginning to show interest in the newborn curled at her feet. With a soft whicker, she nudged the foal, urging the baby stallion to stand and take his first meal.

"She's looking better, Nate." Ben said. "For a while there, I thought I'd lose her. Can't thank you enough."

"Glad I could help." Nate rose from his crouch next to the foal. He'd dried off the newborn and checked him over. So far, so good. "I know what this stallion means to you, Ben, and he's a good-looking fella. Like his daddy."

The horse rancher had lost his registered stallion, a champion quarter horse, to a lightning strike last spring. A couple of months later, he'd been both delighted and nervous to learn his young mare was pregnant for the first time. Knowing that the prized stallion lived on in this foal meant a lot to Ben's livelihood as a horse breeder.

"Not many men would give up a night's sleep for another

man's horse. Calypso's fortunate to have your knowledge and your willingness to lend a hand."

Nate rubbed a hand over the back of his neck and rolled his head back and forth. He remembered another long night with animals, but a certain redhead and a kiss had been included with that one. Unless he counted the nuzzle the mare had given him after he'd helped her baby come into the world, kisses weren't the norm in his world.

"Two years of vet school isn't all that much, but what I learned there and in the school of experience, I'm happy to share. I'm just glad she and her foal are going to make it. Births like this are tricky." One of the foal's legs had been folded back, and the young mare had been nervous, hurting, and scared.

Nate's arms and back ached from fighting against the tide of the mare's contractions to correct the improper presentation, but a sense of satisfaction he couldn't explain to anyone filled his chest. God had made man to be stewards of the animal kingdom, and Nate loved knowing he'd made a difference for both the animal and his neighbor.

The two ranchers stepped out of the stall and walked the length of Ben's horse barn, the scent of horses and alfalfa swirling around them. Valuable animals, purebred stock, stuck their heads over the half-door stalls and watched the human's progress with liquid eyes and soft whickers.

At one end of the barn, Nate stopped at a sink to scrub up. When he finished, Ben clapped him on the back. "How much do I owe you, Nate?"

Nate replaced his hat, left above the sink on a hook while he delivered the foal. "Not a thing. Pay it forward. Or, if you prefer, make a donation to my church. We're raising funds for the after-school program."

"Consider it done and stay for breakfast. Nelly's cooking pancakes."

He was hungry. Near starving after the energy he'd exerted, but Whitney's kitchen, not Ben's, appeared in his thoughts.

"Thanks for the invite, but I'd better get to work." At Whitney's ranch. Preferably at her scarred kitchen table with the twins playing around his legs and Whitney looking too pretty to be real as she scrambled those jelly bean eggs into a tasty omelet.

Ben laughed. "You've been at work since one this morning."

Nate waved as he headed for his truck. Being with Whitney didn't count as work.

Yeah, he was getting in over his head, though he'd managed to keep his growing feelings to himself. Whitney had been crystal clear about her intentions. One year on Sally's ranch, one year to make it legally hers, and she would sell out and hit the road, head to the city where she belonged.

Calypso was only a stopping place, and he was only her neighbor. If he hadn't long ago decided that he and relationships didn't work, he'd be worried that he would crash and burn again when she left.

He pulled into her potholed driveway and mentally kicked himself. The next time he was nearby on the tractor, he'd fix this road before they both lost a wheel in the holes.

He killed the engine, eager to see her, to share his latest adventure. She'd want to know about the baby stallion and how he'd manipulated the bent leg into place.

Whitney opened the front door, and Nate experienced that sudden loss of air pressure, the dip in internal altitude that occurred every single morning. Couldn't be the ranch air. He lived on a ranch. It had to be the redhead.

The babies appeared, one each side of her, chattering something. Sophia spotted him and reached her arms toward him. He loped up the sloping lawn and onto the porch to pick her up. The tiny girl leaned in with a body hug. Honey sweet. Enough to melt the hardest man.

And he'd always been a soft touch.

"Her hands are sticky," Whitney said, too late.

"I'll live. When you hear where I've been all night, you won't worry about sticky fingers."

She didn't pry, and he was a little puzzled. Usually, she was eager for his stories. Wasn't she curious in the least? Didn't she wonder if he'd been out on the town? Or was he such a loser that another woman never crossed her mind?

Inside the kitchen, she handed him a damp cloth. He wiped the baby's hands first and then his sticky cheek.

The place smelled like bacon, and he saw a crispy stack on a plate next to a bowl of pancake batter.

"Pancakes okay?" She poured batter onto a hot skillet. The sound and smell sizzled. His belly growled loud enough to make her smile.

He wouldn't gripe if she fed him mud pies, though he'd had his mouth set for her southwestern style omelet. "Pancakes are fine."

"I have plenty of eggs if you'd rather."

"How about both? I'm hungry."

"I figured." She flashed him a smile, and his stomach dipped. He was doing the one thing he'd promised never to do again. He was falling in love. Not that she was anything like Alicia, other than being a city girl. Alicia had never planned to live on a ranch. But then, come to think of it, neither had Whitney. She was only here for the inheritance.

Maybe the two women had more in common that he wanted to believe, and he was being a fool again.

"What's that scowl for?" She squinted at him, a shiny metal spatula aloft like a weapon.

He intentionally brightened his expression. "Better?"

She cocked a hip. "If you're too busy today, I can handle things. I've already imposed on your good nature too long."

The scowl returned, and he didn't try to hide it. Was she trying to ditch him? "I'm here because I want to be."

She let that soak in, her expression thoughtful. He had no idea what she was thinking. Probably that he was a grumpy old cowboy. Maybe she wanted him to go home and leave her alone.

"If I'm bothering you—"

"You're not," she said. "I don't want to be a burden."

"I thought we were friends. Friends are never a burden."

She turned back to the stove and dished up a tall steaming stack and set it in front of him. He poured warmed syrup over them while she cracked eggs into a bowl and made stirring sounds.

"You don't have to feed me."

"I like to. But if you don't want me to cook for you—"

With a sigh, he shoved the plate away, appetite still there but definitely flagging. "I think we need to talk."

She got a frightened doe look about her. "About what?

"You and me." There, he'd said it. The next move was hers.

"Are you mad at me about something?"

"No."

"Then eat your breakfast before it gets cold." She

pointed the spatula at his stomach. "We can talk after your belly quits growling."

Since she put it that way, he dug in, but the thought of talking about *us* rolled around in his head like a renegade pinball.

Whitney cooked his omelet while he consumed the fluffy pancakes and sneaked bites to two little bird mouths standing at his knee as if she never fed them. Both girls would be sticky again, but he'd clean them up.

When she'd refreshed his coffee and plated the omelet, she took the chair across from him. "All I can cook is breakfast."

He wasn't sure what he'd expected her to say, but it wasn't that. "I'm not complaining."

"You never complain, Nate. You just work. And work. My guess is you worked last night."

Was he that boring and predicable? No hint of mystery whatsoever? "Ben Stallings's mare was in foal."

She folded her hands beneath her chin, interested. He'd told her the story of how God had blessed the rancher with the pregnant mare after the tragedy with his stallion.

"She had trouble? Is she all right?"

"We got her through it. Mom and baby are fine. The foal is a stallion that looks a lot like his sire. Ben was delighted." He put his fork down. "Good man. I'm happy for him."

She reached across the small square table and covered his hand with hers. He felt the sensation of her touch all the way to the toes of his boots. Heart music tuned up like the Boston Pops Symphony.

"You're a good man, too, Nate Caldwell."

That's all it took from her. One touch, and he was messed up. Even when they brushed accidentally in the barn or out in the pasture, his nerve endings reacted like he'd grabbed hold of a frayed electric cord.

He regained his fork, trying to appear nonchalant. "Folks around Calypso help each other. I've been on the receiving end a few times."

With a disbelieving huff, she leaned back. "Name one."

He finished the omelet in two bites. "Sure you want to hear this?"

He wasn't much for talking about Alicia, but she'd already trusted him with her story. Turnabout was fair play.

"I wouldn't have asked if I didn't." She lifted one of the twins onto her lap and wiped Nate's syrup off the baby's face and hands. With twins, he guessed she always kept a wet cloth handy.

He cleared his throat, stretched his hands out on the table top and heaved a sigh. "I always wanted kids. My ex-wife didn't, a little fact she didn't bother to tell me until we miscarried. I was crushed and heartbroken. She was glad to have an excuse to leave. I didn't know she was already seeing someone else." Dumb cowboy. That's what Alicia had called him. Dumb, clueless country bumpkin.

She turned his hand over and laced her fingers with his. "I understand that kind of hurt."

Some of his tension ebbed.

"I know you do." He saw his reflection in her blue eyes, the elements of sorrow and loss and the shock of knowing failure. He'd recovered from Alicia's betrayal, but not the loss of the child. Whether it had carried his DNA or not, he'd wanted that baby. "For a while after she left, I was so low, I could have crawled under a snake's belly and quit breathing, but Calypso wouldn't let me."

"What did they do?"

He chuckled, remembering. "Nearly worked me to death. Every time I'd get gloomy, my phone would ring. I suspect Connie and Emily had a lot to do with that. Some tried to fix me up with dates." He titled his head in a comic pose, eyebrow jacked. "I refused those, but a few were intended to make me smile. One was with old Mrs. Pearson who is at least ninety and hasn't had a lucid thought since she was sixty."

Whitney laughed and then sobered. "Poor lady. I shouldn't have laughed."

"Go ahead. I laughed too. But I took her some flowers at the rest home, and she asked me to marry her. I said she was too good for me, and she agreed. We parted friends."

They both laughed again, the mood lightening as he went on, "Others wanted my opinion on a mare or a cow or the color they should paint their barn. I think I helped paint six barns in two months. Not to mention the fence I built, the fishing holes I fished, and the calves I worked, all with a friend or relative right next to me filling me with wisdom and good humor. I wanted to go somewhere like an old worn out bull and die, but they wouldn't leave me alone long enough to do it."

"Keeping busy helped me too. If I hadn't had the twins, I'm not sure how I would have survived."

Unlike him, she didn't mention friends and family to help her through the loss. Again, he realized how blessed he was.

He also realized she was still holding his hand and decided he wouldn't mind sitting here all day. If that made him a fool, he guessed he was one. But maybe that was as far as he should take it for now.

"About us," he said. "I liked kissing you."

Not a good start, Caldwell. One thing for sure, he'd never be a silver-tongued Don Juan.

"I wondered." She started to pull her hand away, but he held fast.

"Wouldn't mind trying it again sometime."

She blushed. "Me, either."

"Well, then." He stood, slowly bringing her up with him. The twins patted at his legs and jabbered, but for once, he ignored them.

She followed him up, her light blue eyes never leaving his face. Her chest rose and fell as her pupils dilated, the black centers pushing the blue out to the rim.

"I know you've been hurt."

"You too." Her breath tickled the skin on his face, raised his yearning a good two notches. "But a kiss between friends is safe, isn't it?"

Friends? Not hardly. But if he didn't kiss her, he'd implode right here on her white linoleum floor, so he locked onto her suggestion. "Whatever you say. However you want to play it."

But he wasn't playing at all. And the realization jarred him. Whitney Brookes was shaking him out of his lethargy, no matter what she wanted to call it.

"I like that idea. Kissing friends." Her answer was a whisper as her bottom lip dropped open.

He could no more resist that invitation than he could resist her omelets. As gently as he knew how, as if she were one of his flighty mares, he cupped her face and pressed his mouth to hers. She shivered, and he took that as a good sign, wrapping his arms around her until they were as close as a thought.

He breathed her in, a mix of bacon and sunshine, and

deepened the kiss until his knees went shaky and the heart music started playing. Reluctantly, he broke the kiss, but not his embrace. He could stand right here in her kitchen with her slender arms holding him close from now on and not ever get hungry again. Except for her. His good, good friend.

He studied her pretty face, all pink and cream and long pale lashes. A man could get used to that face across his breakfast table every morning. And on his pillow every night.

He caught himself up short. There he went again, forgetting everything he'd learned the hard way. Though the idea chafed against him worse than cheap boots, Whitney only wanted friendship, and her way was for the best. All he had of Whitney and the twins was a year. Less, now that two months had passed and winter crept in like a burglar threatening to steal her away.

Less than a year to be with her, to care for her, to love on those little girls and show them what a daddy was supposed to be. To show her how a real man loves.

To convince her that staying was better than leaving.

But this time he knew the score. This time, he'd be prepared for the day she drove away with his heart.

IT WAS ONLY a kiss between neighborly friends. No reason to go all junior high school and swoon over a big, sexy cowboy with a heart the size of his ranch. But that's the way Whitney felt as she strolled across the green lawn, holding Nate's hand on one side and Olivia's on the other. Sophia had attached herself to the cowboy on the opposite end until they looked like a game of Red Rover.

Her mouth still tingled from the passionate kiss that

didn't feel anything like a friendly peck. If she'd been wearing socks, Nate would have knocked them off.

For a tired man who'd been up most of the night, he'd retained plenty of energy. Wow, did he ever! She was amazed at all he did and understood now why he'd been so reluctant in the beginning to help on her ranch. Not counting his own horses and cattle, the man was in high demand all the time.

He'd delivered Ben's colt last night. Two days ago, he and the pastor had built a wheelchair ramp on Mr. Jacob's back porch so the older gentleman could get his wife in and out. Last week, somebody's dog got hit by a car. Before that, he and Gilbert had erected a new sign at the church and patched a leaky roof.

She slid a glance his way, admiring his profile and the way he dipped sideways now and then to listen to her daughter and make her giggle.

The man absolutely stopped her breath with the way he adored her girls. Nate would make a great father.

She caught the direction of her thoughts and reeled them in like a fishing line tossed out too far. Some places she simply could not let herself go. Nate was a friend and neighbor. Two kisses didn't indicate a relationship or even a desire for one. Plain and simple, a man who could kiss like simply *had* to kiss someone.

Suddenly, Nate stopped walking and yanked Whitney out of her teenage daydream. "Did you leave that gate open on purpose?"

"What gate?" Before he could reply, she saw the opening to one of the pastures. "Oh, no."

She broke the connection of hands and jogged toward the sheep pasture, hoping like mad that none of the baby doll sheep were on the loose. "How did this happen? I'm positive I shut that gate."

Nate, with the twins hot on his heels, went around her to look across the fenced field. "I don't see anything out there, but they could be back in the woods or lying down by the creek."

Whitney spun toward the barn, pulse jumping like crickets in a forest fire. "Yesterday, something got into the barn and knocked over some feed. I wonder—"

She'd blamed Clive at first, but he'd been right where she'd put him, along with the other horses. The donkeys and cows weren't responsible, either, which left yesterday's spilled feed a mystery. And now another gate left open.

"You check the barn," Nate said. "I'll walk the fence and see if I can find any sign of the sheep."

He was gone in a flash, strong legs eating up the ground between the barn and the big pasture. He probably wished for a real horse at a time like this, and maybe she needed one to keep up with this many critters, especially since they seemed to be conspiring against her.

"I go. I go, too. I go!" Jumping up and down, Olivia chose that moment to declare her preference for the cowboy, and when she didn't get her way, the toddler set up a howl that startled the goats. Three of them fainted.

With Olivia yowling and Sophia beginning to sniffle in sisterly sympathy, Whitney's journey to the barn was slow and torturous. By the time she'd checked all the feed rooms and found them undisturbed, Nate was back.

Olivia, drama queen in training, threw herself at his legs and squealed. "My Nate! Mine."

Out of breath from the jog, he patted her ponytails, but his attention was on Whitney. "I counted fifteen sheep in the pasture with the donkeys and horses. That's all of them, right?"

"Yes. But how did they get back there? Was the gate into the horse pasture open too?"

"No." He removed his hat and scratched at the back of his head. "You sure you didn't get distracted and leave the gates open even for a few minutes?"

"I don't think so." But that's what she'd done before, wasn't it?

After much thought and retracing her every moment in the barnyard, she'd come to the conclusion that she'd been the guilty party when Billy, the goat, had escaped. Yet, she didn't recall opening that gate. Or closing it.

"Maybe I did, Nate." She told him about the other incident. "I must have been opening the gate when Sophia cried out, and I ran to her without securing the latch."

"It happens. Human kids are more important than goat kids."

She tried to smile, grateful for his understanding. That was Nate. Kind to everyone and everything.

She glanced at those perfect lips, now in a flat line of concern, and wished to turn back time to the kitchen. For that too brief moment in his arms, she'd experience more comfort and security than she'd had in months. Years, actually. Not to mention the riot of romantic notions still skating through her bloodstream and dancing on her nerve endings. A woman didn't easily forget a kiss like that.

"Sally's lawyer was here at the time." She gently pushed the kiss to the back burner, where it remained fully ignited. "I don't think he approves of me as Sally's heir. For sure, he doesn't think I can handle this farm, and maybe he's right. Sometimes I feel so inadequate."

Nate glanced away, staring at the row of barn stalls, a scowl on his face as deep as her driveway ruts. "Does that mean you're giving up? Going back to St. Louis?"

If the statement hadn't been so impossible, she would have laughed. He didn't know, and she wasn't about to tell him, that she had nothing but a homeless shelter to go back to.

"This is my inheritance. Mine and Olivia's and Sophia's. No matter her reasons, Sally wanted us to have it. And I intend to do all I can to finish out this year successfully and claim this ranch as mine."

For some reason, her words didn't have the impact she'd expected. Nate's head bobbed once and, without meeting her eyes, he clapped his hat back on and said, "Let's get busy then. Sheep won't move themselves, and the water troughs are empty."

"That's impossible. I refilled them last night." She scooped up the girls and hurried to keep up with him as they exited the barn. "Did I say something to make you mad?"

He looked at her but kept walking. "You sure those troughs were full?"

"Positive."

His scowl returned, but this time she knew it wasn't for her. "Then, how?"

Whitney gnawed her bottom lip. Had she forgotten? Was she that distracted? That inadequate?

Finally, she admitted. "I don't know."

11

Over the next several weeks, a worrisome thought nagged at Nate and grew in intensity. He'd wrangled and wrestled the problems at Whitney's ranch every which direction trying to come up with a reasonable explanation but had found none.

Or maybe he was over-thinking the situation, afraid of failing Whitney like he'd failed Alicia. As his ex had reminded him all too often, he could be as dense as the Amazon Forest. Too little, too late, a cowboy with his head stuck in a barn, unable to see the clues and act in time. He didn't want to be guilty of that with Whitney.

At least once a week since the sheep incident, something went awry at Whitney's farm. At first, he'd thought the greenhorn city girl was either an absentminded klutz or a too-busy mama who had too much on her plate to look after a hundred animals. But now, he was having second thoughts. And third ones, too. Whitney was conscientious, a hard worker. A real good kisser, too, but he didn't share that with his brother and Gilbert, both of whom agreed something at Whitney's place seemed fishy. Was it her? Or was it something else?

The three men and Connie were in the Triple C living room, the TV on mute while the guys talked and sipped after-dinner coffee, and Connie created magic with her knitting needles. Emily had stopped by earlier, but she'd had a meeting tonight. City council or some such. His sister was always busy.

Nate propped his sock feet on the ottoman and sipped at his mug, glad for the warmth. The nights were almost cool enough now to build a fire in the fireplace and toast s'mores. He'd bet his boots the twins would love that. So would Whitney.

"Yesterday, I shut and locked the tack room myself," he said. "This morning, the door was open, and every chicken on the place was inside."

He didn't have to explain the damage a chicken could do to leather. Whitney had nearly cried when she'd stepped inside, but she'd sent his admiration skyrocketing when she hadn't. With her chin quivering, she'd rounded up the fuzzy-headed chickens and then marched to the house for warm water and rags and gotten busy with the cleanup.

"Did Whitney say if she'd gone back out to the barn last night after you left?" Gilbert asked.

"She hadn't. Sophia had a stomach virus. Whitney didn't leave her for a minute." This morning she had looked as gray as warmed-over gravy, but the toddler had finally been asleep and feeling better.

"Why did she not call me? I would go and help. Emily too. We are her friends." Connie jabbed a knitting needle at the yarn with particular indignation. "Is the *bebe* better today?"

"I stopped by her place before I came home for dinner. Baby is up and running. A little fussy but on the mend."

"Good. Good. But this trouble. *That* is not good." Connie's needled dipped and jabbed through pink yarn. He didn't need to be a genius to know the garment was for one of the twins.

"Maybe I should give Lawson a call tomorrow." Lawson Hawk was the county sheriff and a lifelong friend. "He'll run out and make an assessment. Whitney should get acquainted with him, anyway."

Gilbert lifted an eyebrow. "Sure you want the sheriff visiting your girl? He's got a reputation with the ladies."

"She's not my girl." Nate refused to be jealous of a good friend, even one who was every bit as single and a lot better looking.

Gilbert laughed. He had a bad habit of doing that. If he didn't agree or thought you were being stupid, he didn't say a word. He just laughed.

Connie looked up from her knitting. "She and the twins must move in with us until this is settled."

Nate nearly spit his coffee. "What?"

"For her own good. If someone is trying to scare her away, she could get hurt." Connie nailed him with her black eyes. "I will fix up the two end rooms by yours."

Nate considered this both the best and worst idea Connie had ever had. "I'm not sure the situation is that serious, Connie. Besides, she wouldn't accept. She has to live on the property to inherit."

The year thing still stuck in his craw like a sideways chicken bone, but right now, his concern was for her and the twins. She wanted that ranch, and no one was going to take it from her.

"If she is in danger—"

"We don't know that, Connie." Ace leaned up, letting his sock feet drop to the floor. All of them were bootless, knowing to shuck their footwear in the mudroom or face a fiery rebuke, most of which would be in Spanish, but even a man who didn't speak the language would get her drift. "This may be a case of teenagers playing pranks."

"Or maybe someone has a crush on Whitney and is trying to get her attention." Gilbert nodded sagely. "She's a mighty fine looking woman."

Nate's thoughts shot to L.T. Jenkins. He hadn't come around again, as far as Nate knew. Was he vindictive enough to pay Whitney's farm nighttime visits to open gates, empty troughs, dump out feed, and bust bales of hay?

Nah. A grown man didn't have time for that kind of nonsense. Did he?

The TV flickered as programming changed and someone tried to sell him a slicer-dicer for only nineteen dollars and ninety-five cents. Outside, the moon had risen and darkness slouched in, a blanket over the earth.

He removed his cell phone and stared at Whitney's number, thinking to call her. Better to overreact than to let something happen. "Maybe I should take a run over every night after supper and have a look around."

The other three exchanged looks.

"Good idea, Nate. Go now." Connie made a shooing motion with her needles. "Take some cake."

With a wry smile, he shook his head, but on his way out, he stopped by the kitchen for a giant slice of Connie's chocolate-cinnamon cake.

WHITNEY HEARD a vehicle and put down her pen to look outside. The familiar mahogany GMC rumbled to a stop.

Nate. Her heart lifted. That he'd been here a few hours ago mattered little. She couldn't wait to see him again.

That was her problem. She'd shot right past the friend label and moved to romance and maybe even love. She was an idiot, one who fell hard and fast and made colossal mistakes. Even now, when she told herself to be cool, to keep an arm's length, every nerve ending danced to know Nate was headed her direction.

He'd never stopped by this late before. Had he forgotten something? She flashed back to the night of the fire. Had something happened?

She hurried to flip on the light as he stepped up on the porch. Her heart leapt, yearned, and refused to settle. There were regular men and then there were real men. Nate Caldwell was the latter.

"Nate?" She kept her voice low so the girls wouldn't awaken. "Is everything all right?"

"That's what I came to ask you." He removed his hat and stood outside the old-fashioned storm door looking serious. The yellow bug light turned him golden.

"You could have called." But she was so glad he was here in the flesh. That she could not only hear his voice, she could see his face and touch him. Oh, she longed to touch him, to throw herself into his arms and tell him she didn't want to be his friend anymore.

"Am I bothering you?"

Not in the way he meant.

"Course not." She pushed at the screen. "The babies are asleep."

"Okay." He stepped quietly inside, filling the room with

his presence and the clean scent of outdoors that seemed to cling to his skin and clothes. "You busy?"

"Trying to create better records." Sally's haphazard method of recording births, deaths, purchases, and sales hadn't been too accurate. According to Nate's wise advice, she needed good records for tax purposes as well as for her own use. "One of the nannies gave birth to twins a bit ago. If you hadn't told me to look in on her, I would have missed an amazing sight."

As always, Nate's assessment had been spot-on. She truly did not know what she would do without him, and the thought of even trying scared her in a way she couldn't explain. But it was more than his ranching knowledge. It was him. She knew better than to let her heart get involved, but as her family would confirm, when had she ever listened to common sense?

"She had twins?" Nate held his hat by the indented crown and placed the gray Stetson on an end table before he settled on Sally's saggy old couch. "Did she have any trouble?"

"I would have called you if she had. It was a wonderful experience. I'm still floating on air."

She'd wanted to call him and share in the moment, but she'd held herself firmly in check. The last thing she wanted was to drive him away with her neediness.

"Pretty special stuff, seeing new life come into the world."

She stuck her hands in her back pockets and smiled. She'd known Nate would understand. "Want to see them?"

He stood and glanced toward the short hall leading to the bedrooms. "The twins okay?"

"Shouldn't wake up until morning. They've slept well since we moved here."

"What about you?" He held the door for her, his head tilted to look at her. "How do you like country nights?"

Shorter by several inches, Whitney slipped under the arc of his raised arm, accidentally brushing his body as she passed into the light of the porch. Nate closed the door carefully, gently, so as not to wake the girls.

The air was crisp, a warning of soon coming frost, and Whitney crossed her arms against the cool. "Love the nights now that I've gotten used to the noises."

Darkness lay across the lawn and driveway between the house and barn. Shadowy buildings rose like specters, and white moonlight glinted off metal gates and fences. At first, the noises and darkness and stark aloneness had spooked her, but now, she loved everything about her little ranch. Often, after the babies were in bed, she sat on the porch, awestruck by the glittery night sky, and talked to God.

"Noises?" Nate cocked his head, amused. "Country is quiet."

"To you maybe." She crossed her arms against the chilly air.

"Are you cold?"

"I should have grabbed a sweater."

"And take away my excuse to do this?" He draped an arm over her shoulders and pulled her close to his side.

He didn't need an excuse, but she didn't tell him that.

She snuggled in, breathed the essence of cotton shirt and shower soap, and felt...valued, womanly. "Forget what I said about the sweater."

His laugh was soft against her hair. "I'm glad you don't mind. I was about to die to touch you."

He was?

"You're so warm." A ridiculous thing to say, but his admission flustered her.

"You're so small."

She laughed. "Average maybe."

"You feel small to a man. Holding you makes me feel strong and capable. I like the feeling."

She liked it too. A lot. Just as she liked him. When he turned her sideways in the moonlight, still sheltering her with his warmth, she was ready for his kiss. Never mind that the imp tapping at the back of her brain warned of impending doom.

Their lips met in a gentle seeking, soft and pleasurable, but a hint of passion lurked around the edges. At some point, one of them took the kiss up a notch, deepening the intensity, melding them. Had it been her?

In his embrace, Whitney's world, out of control for years, began to center and settle. This, of course, made absolutely no sense. After all the mistakes she'd made, she knew better to let another man into her life. Especially now when she couldn't afford complications that might interfere with securing a home and a future for the twins.

But for this brief instant, cocooned by this gentle, thoughtful man, she was no longer afraid.

Around them, night pulsed and animals rustled. A dove cooed from the barn loft while they explored this most interesting friendship that had led to more and more kisses each time they met.

He claimed they were friends, but the heart-melting cowboy with his kind ways and warm kisses was coming to mean so much more to Whitney.

Sometimes, like now, she thought they needed to talk.

That she needed to get her feelings out into the open. But fear held her back. He'd been hurt, too, and he'd been clear that he only wanted a friend with kissing benefits. Friends who liked to be together, who liked to talk and laugh together. Only friends.

What if he didn't want anything except these stolen kisses in the moonlight? What if he rejected her now that she'd begin to love him? Could she bear that kind of loss again?

Better to keep him as a friend than lose him altogether.

HE WAS IN TOO DEEP. He was going to get his heart shredded into coleslaw.

Slowly, Nate untangled his mouth from Whitney's and, breathing like a race horse at the end of the Derby, kept her close as they went inside the barn to see the new twin goats.

He'd been telling the truth when he said he was dying to touch her. He loved holding her in his arms and kissing her warm, honeyed mouth. He loved the way she made his knees weak. He loved the tremble that shivered through her body.

He loved the rest of her too. Her grit and determination to succeed. Her laughter and the way her nose wrinkled when she encountered a disgusting barnyard odor. The way she mothered her children. The way she'd gone out of her way to sit beside the smelly, shabby homeless man who snuck into the back of the church service last Sunday.

Yeah, that had really gotten him.

He just plain loved Whitney Brookes.

Connie's matchmaking schemes to bring them together

were unnecessary. He couldn't stay away from Whitney if his life depended on it.

"They're in the third stall," she was saying.

Reluctantly, he released his hold to open the stall door. Inside, a pair of spotted kids no bigger than puppies staggered around their black-and-white mother, stiff legs splayed wide for balance.

"They look healthy." Nate checked over the nanny, running a soothing hand down her back. She butted gently at his leg.

Assured that all was well with the new kids, he remembered his reason for being here and moved on through the barn and out into the back lot. If someone was sneaking in during the night to cause mischief, he wanted to know.

"Nate?" Whitney followed, the barn light glowing around her until she became a shadow like him. "What are you doing?"

"Just looking around."

"Why?"

"I don't want to scare you."

"You just did." She looped her arm through his and leaned in, face lifted toward him. "What's going on?"

He covered her fingers with his and didn't answer. Eyesight adjusted to the low light of the moon's glow, he scanned the fields all the way to the horizon. Nothing. No car lights. No movement.

He squeezed her fingers. "You've had too many incidents lately. I worry someone is sneaking in here at night."

With a sharp inhale, she moved closer. "Is that why you came over?"

His gaze drifted over her face, to her lips. Was there real

trouble? Or was he simply looking for an excuse to be with his neighbor?

"Not entirely." His mouth curved. "Connie sent cake, which I forgot to take out of the truck."

She skipped right past his attempt at humor. "Why would anyone want to cause trouble for me? And who?"

"Don't know. L.T., maybe? Would you be interested in talking to the sheriff?"

Whitney drew back, expression alarmed. "Do I need to?"

"Yes." He tugged her close again. "I think you do."

SHERIFF LAWSON HAWK was a tall man in a cowboy hat and boots with the thickest black eyelashes and brightest blue eyes Whitney had ever seen on a male.

He arrived the next morning after Nate had come and gone, his sheriff's badge glinting above a scary looking gun and a belt radio that made frequent squawky noises. She supposed in rural areas a radio was more essential than a cell phone.

Whitney pushed the twins in the stroller around the farm while she explained the rash of strange problems. Today, while he was here, everything was as it should be. Naturally. Every animal in its spot. Every door and gate secured. Every feed sack and barrel safe and sound.

To the sheriff's credit, he listened with thoughtful respect and filled out a report. There wasn't much else he could do.

"You've seen no one? Had no problems with any of the neighbors?"

Sophia threw her dolly in the dirt for Whitney to

retrieve. "The Caldwells are my nearest neighbors. They've been great."

"You can't think of anyone you've gotten crossways with? Someone who might want to stir up trouble for you?"

"I haven't been here very long, and I don't think I've made any enemies or upset anyone." Unless she counted the woman Sophia threw up on in the grocery check-out line last week. And the amorous cowboy, L.T., but that had been weeks ago, and she hadn't seen him since. She mentioned the name anyway.

The sheriff shook his head. "Nate told me about the trouble with L.T., but last I heard, he was headed to Wyoming. I'll double-check though, just to be sure."

Whitney rubbed both hands down the thighs of her jeans, as bewildered as the lawman. "Thank you."

"I wish I could do more to help, but there isn't much to go on. Random problems could happen on any farm. Unless an actual crime is committed..." The sheriff let her fill in the blanks. An opened gate or spilled feed wasn't a criminal offense.

Admittedly, she felt a little let down. She'd wasted his time, and he probably pegged her as was one of those hysterical females who call the cops every time they hear a noise or see a shadow. "I understand."

He stuck his pen in the top of the clip board and began walking toward his vehicle, a white SUV with *Calypso County Sheriff* emblazed down the side in green lettering.

The stroller wheels rattled as Whitney bumped alongside him. "I'm sorry I wasted your time coming out here."

She wouldn't bother him again.

A smile crinkled around those fabulous eyelashes. The sheriff probably had women making false reports all the time to get him to stop in and chat. She hoped he didn't think that about her.

"No problem. Nate says you're new at ranching. It's normal to need some time."

So he *did* think she was a silly city girl who'd probably caused her own problems.

At the SUV, he opened the door and turned to her. "No harm in filling out a report. In the future, keep on the look out for tire tracks, footprints, any human activity. If any damage is done, give me a call."

"What about the fire? Wasn't that damaging enough?"

"No indication the fire on Caldwell land was connected to your situation or that it was anything other than a careless accident. Unfortunately, the campfire spot was all we had to go on. If someone is intentionally trying to upset you, they're smart enough not to leave evidence."

Right. A careless accident. She'd seen a lot of careless accidents lately.

After a few more exchanges, Whitney stood in the driveway and watched him leave. The sheriff was professional. He'd done his job, but she could tell he didn't believe anything serious was happening. And maybe it wasn't. She second-guessed herself all the time.

Embarrassed, she pushed the stroller down to the chicken pen for the twins to enjoy their favorite pets. The Polish hens seemed to show off whenever the twins toddled up to the fence and started chattering. Fluffing their feathery crests, the lady chickens raced toward the fence while the rooster she'd named Mick Jagger let rip with a hearty crow. One of the hens stopped in mid-run to stare at Mick as if to say, "What was that?"

Between the chickens and the playful goats, she always

had a reason to smile at her menagerie, even on days when she wanted to cry.

The sheriff was right. No one had a reason to bother her. Nate had been sweet and supportive to take her concerns seriously, but he probably knew it, too. She was simply a bad-luck rancher who had no idea what she was doing.

She squatted behind the girls and listened to their chatter. The ranch was a peaceful, happy, healthy place. Anything bad that happened was her fault, and she wasn't going to say another word to anyone.

12

L ife was good. In fact, life was great. Never mind that she'd lost another sack of feed when two squatty little donkeys invaded the mysteriously opened feed room yesterday afternoon. Whitney was not about to complain. If weird things happened on her farm, she must be responsible.

Just for today, she planned to put all her worries aside and have fun. With Nate and the twins.

As she dressed her daughters in identical purple sweat pants and matching zip hoodies, Whitney hummed a perky tune. Today promised to be awesome. Even if she *was* getting in over her head with a certain cowboy.

Last night, Nate had shown up on her doorstep with a pumpkin so enormous he'd pretended to struggle to carry it into the house. It was his endearing way of inviting her and the twins to a pumpkin patch. They'd had a blast carving the jack-o-lantern, which now decorated her front porch with a lopsided grin and a Magic-Marker mustache.

Yes, life was looking up. God had led her here to

Calypso. He had given her this incredible gift of home and property. And He'd sent a new friend in Emily and a good man to teach her all the things she needed to know about ranching. That she no longer needed Nate's daily help was beside the point. They both knew it, but he kept right on coming over, and she went right on enjoying every moment.

She refused to let spilled feed and opened gates steal her joy. Wasn't that what Pastor Marcus preached on last week?

Setting the girls on their feet, she lovingly swatted each bottom just as she heard the rumble of Nate's truck pulling into the drive. Both girls squealed and headed for the door.

Nate exited the truck, and Whitney held back her own squeal. In black hat and shirt, he looked ruggedly fit and splendidly sexy.

Whitney pushed the storm door open and turned the bouncing girls loose. They made a beeline for the cowboy. He lifted them both, one in each muscular arm.

"Look what I found running loose." He grinned at Whitney. "You guys ready?"

"Let me grab their bag and lock up. We'll need their car seats out of the Subaru."

"I'm on it."

By the time she crossed the yard to his truck, Nate was buckling the last twin into her safety seat. He patted the baby's leg and slammed the door.

"Now." Grinning, he leaned in and kissed her. "Hi."

A little tickle of pleasure lifted the corners of her mouth. "You're in a happy mood."

"The best." He escorted her around the truck and opened the passenger side. When Whitney started to step up into the high cab, strong hands gripped her waist and lifted her easily into the seat. "It's not every day I have three beautiful girls in my truck, a perfect day off, and good times ahead. Gotta make the most of it."

With a wink, he kissed her on the nose and jogged around to the driver's side. Fluttery, excited, and a little bit flustered, Whitney settled back and listened to his funny tale about Gilbert and a mad mama cow while they drove the twenty miles to the Kinsey Farm Pumpkin Patch.

The result was worth the drive. Besides the inevitable stacks and stacks of bright orange pumpkins, the patch boasted a corn maze, hayrides, pumpkin decorating, face painting, and more. A perfect family outing.

Not that Nate was family.

They'd no more than entered the wooden gates than Nate pointed to a pair of *your-face-here* cutouts of cartoon farmers in overalls and straw hats. "Photo-op. You take the picture. I'll hold the girls."

He scooped a child into each arm and somehow managed to get their tiny, giggling faces through the holes while Whitney snapped photos with the cell phone.

"Our turn," she said.

Nate gave a mock scowl, a child now attached to each leg. "I'm a rancher, not a farmer."

"Not today." Laughing, Whitney gave him a little push and handed the phone to an obliging stranger.

When they emerged from behind the cutouts to reclaim the camera, the older woman returned the device to Nate.

"I love seeing a dad enjoying time with his children." She patted Sophia's head. "You have a beautiful family. You're a lucky man."

Nate didn't flinch. In his usual polite way, he took the camera and nodded. "Yes, ma'am, I sure am. Thank you."

The woman thought they were husband and wife. That

Nate was the twins' father. And if Whitney entertained the thought a little too long, no one knew but her.

As they walked away, she snuck a peak at Nate. He winked and reached for her hand. Almost giddy, she grinned and laced her fingers with his. Neither mentioned the woman's error, but it lingered in the air, an unspoken temptation.

The twins, ponytails bobbing, rushed ahead to touch and explore every flower, pumpkin, and bale of hay. Occasionally, they paused to jabber at another child and squeal in sheer delight.

When she was with Nate, Whitney had the same reaction. She knew better, but when had she ever been wise in the love department?

Love. The word immobilized her. Disarmed her. She couldn't fall in love. Love hurt too much.

But somehow, this feeling she had for Nate didn't hurt at all. It felt really, really good.

In front of her, Nate stopped and turned around, clearly wondering why she'd frozen like a Popsicle. "You get lost?"

Whitney gave a self-conscious laugh. "This is such a great place. I was just...admiring it." And you.

Hands on his hips, considering, he looked around at the various activities underway. "You could do something similar."

"Really? You think so?" She latched on to the idea, trying her best to forget that pesky love word.

"Why not? It fits right in with your other plans. All you need that you don't already have is pumpkins. You could plant and raise them yourself or buy in bulk from a local farmer."

"That's true, but I don't have one of those." She pointed

at a tractor pulling a wagonload of visitors around an open field. "And I can't afford to buy one."

"You have something better. A pony cart. And there's harness in the tack room and an old wagon in the barn. We can paint it a bright color, toss in a few bales of hay, and you should be good to go."

"That's a really good idea." She liked how he'd said *we* would paint the wagon. "Not that Clive is going to be too happy pulling a cart."

"Cantankerous Clive aside, you have plenty of other horses, donkeys too, that can be trained to do the job. It's not that hard."

"Says the lifetime horseman."

Whitney lifted a climbing Olivia onto a hay bale. The toddler promptly flopped on her belly, slid back down and reached her hands up to go again. Bits of hay stuck to her sweat pants. Whitney absently dusted it off.

"But seeing how successful this pumpkin patch is, I'm game to try it. Selling my extra livestock isn't enough income, and my goat-soap project will take some time to get off the ground, but if I can add this and a year-round petting zoo, I should be able to make a living."

"You could host other seasonal events, too."

Sophie reached for Nate, and he set her on the hay bales. With a shout of laughter, she slid to the ground and lifted her arms again.

"Like what?"

"I don't know. Let's think." Without missing a beat, Nate reloaded the toddler. "Christmas is major. What about wagon rides with Santa and a story time?"

"Kind of a farmer's version of The Polar Express?" She loved it!

"Invest a little in outdoor decorations, lights, etc. Serve hot cocoa and candy canes."

Excited, Whitney threw both hands in the air. "Oh, oh, oh! Another idea. Open the barn up for an indoor petting zoo, and put antlers on the goats and red bows on the sheep. We can take pictures of the kids with the animals."

"And load the results on your website for download as souvenirs."

Some of her excitement fizzled. "I don't have a website."

"Putting one together is not that hard. I can show you. Emily too."

The excitement returned and brought a friend.

"Oh, my goodness. Oh, my goodness. This is awesome!" Whitney clapped her hands and hopped up and down, drawing laughter from the twins, both of whom hopped and clapped in imitation and then giggled at each other.

People would come. She knew they would. Families with children, school and church groups, city folks looking for the country life.

"I get excited thinking about all the possibilities."

"As far as I know, there's nothing similar anywhere in Calypso County. Individual things like this, yes." He dipped his chin toward the pumpkin patch. "But nothing like what you have in mind."

A mix of fear and anticipation jittered in her belly. She was starting to want this badly. Wanting something too much was always a bad sign. She still had months to go to prove herself as Sally's heir. What if she ventured out and failed and lost the ranch altogether? Failure was the only thing she'd ever been good at.

But maybe, just maybe, with God as her guide and a

little imagination and lots of hard work, her miniature petting zoo and events farm would be a big success.

While she daydreamed, the twins spotted a giant inflated bouncy house where a dozen other children screamed and jumped. Running at full tilt to reach the toy, Olivia stumbled and went down. Before Whitney could react, Nate was there to set the toddler on her feet and inspect outstretched palms for scrapes. Olivia shuddered in a sniffle, threatening to cry. The cowboy murmured something, Olivia thrust out both hands, and he planted a kiss on each palm.

"You're okay, ladybug." He pulled Olivia against him for a quick hug. "Nate's got you."

Small arms encircled the man's neck. He lifted the toddler onto one knee and dusted grass from her pant legs. She responded with a baby kiss on his cheek. Sophia, not to be left-out, squeezed into the circle of love and held out both palms—which Nate promptly kissed.

Whitney thought she would melt like chocolate on a hot s'more. Her little girls. The manly cowboy. If ever she'd experienced a family feeling, it was today with her twins and Nate.

She wondered if he felt it too because his eyes met hers over the girls' heads. Quiet, steady. Like his personality. Whitney held on as long as she could, but the twins broke the moment. Now loved and healed, they wiggled down and continued their trek to the bouncy house.

Love. Family. Nate. This sunny October day was getting to her.

After the bounce house, the foursome got lost in the corn maze, and Whitney laughed at Nate's silly "escape" antics until her sides hurt. When the twins tired of the dizzying game, piggy back rides solved the problem. She and Nate trotted like horses through the labyrinth, laughing, teasing.

Happy. She was happy. Whitney slid a glance toward the cowboy, thankful he'd come into her life.

After the maze, they rode in the wagon, milked a pretend cow, fed bottles to baby goats—an activity that gave Whitney more ideas for her farm—and finally let the girls each choose a tiny pumpkin to take home.

"I'm starved," Nate announced as he started the truck engine. "Still up for the Burger Barn?"

The twins sat happily in their car seats slurping sippy cups, eyes droopy and legs kicking.

"They'll probably fall asleep before we get there."

"Want to go home, then?"

"No."

He grinned over at her. "Hoping you'd say that."

"Today was fun."

"It's not over yet."

She liked the sound of that.

CALYPSO'S BURGER BARN, which bore no resemblance whatsoever to a barn, smelled of grilled onions and sizzling meat. Whitney's stomach growled the moment they walked in the door.

A blond woman of considerable girth and over six feet tall barreled toward them with fleshy arms outstretched. "Nate, you old dog! Where you been?"

While Whitney looked on, amused, the blonde pounded Nate's back hard enough to loosen a lung.

He laughed and returned the hug, lifting her slightly off

the floor. "Much as I love your company, Aunt Mint, a man's got to make a living."

Aunt Mint's laugh was as big as her body, and that was saying plenty.

She turned her attention to Whitney. "Who is this pretty redhead you've found? And what's she doing with the likes of you?"

Nate made the introductions. "This is my neighbor, Whitney Brookes."

Aunt Mint stuck out a beefy hand and pumped Whitney's arm. "A real pleasure to make your acquaintance. Sally, God rest her, was a dear soul. I'm sorry for your loss."

"Thank you." No point explaining the relationship, or lack thereof, she had with Sally Rogers. Sally had given her a farm. She was, indeed, a dear soul.

"Who are these darling little girls? Twins, aren't they?" The woman asked. "Cute as pie."

Nate dropped a wide palm on each little head. "These are Olivia and Sophia. Sophia has the pink ribbons."

Awestruck, both girls had their dark heads tilted back as far as they could in order to stare wide-eyed at the big woman.

"Look at those big, pretty, black eyes." The massive Mint couldn't bend too far, certainly not as far down as the babies, but she patted the tops of their heads and shouted to a waitress. "Sam Ella, these twinkies need the baby special and a pair of high chairs."

Sam Ella, a brunette as thin as Aunt Mint was thick, rounded up the chairs and helped settle the twins, handing them each a small plastic toy and a mini-pack of animal crackers.

Once the adults were seated with water and menus,

Whitney leaned toward Nate. "Why do you call her Aunt Mint?"

"That's her name."

"Her name is Aunt?"

Nate's mouth curved. "No, her name is Mint, but she's kin to half the town and the other half owes her money, so everyone calls her Aunt Mint."

"Which one are you?"

He laughed. "At one time I was both. We're distant cousins of some kind. Her great-great granddaddy and mine were brothers."

"Does that get you a burger discount?"

"Not hardly, but on good days, she has been known to toss in a few extra fries."

"Let's hope this is a good day."

Nate laughed. "Hungry, are you?"

Sam Ella returned and took their order. Nate ordered extra fries, his brown eyes laughing at Whitney the whole time.

When the waitress left, Whitney leaned back in her chair and sighed, tired but content in a way she could not have imagined a few months ago.

"Good day?" Nate ripped open Olivia's animal crackers and handed the baby an elephant cookie.

"Right now, the world feels perfect. I haven't had this much fun in forever." Not since long before the babies.

"We should do it again. I mean, take the girls on outings. Babies need experiences for healthy growth and development." He shifted, looking uncomfortable. "That sounded stupid, but it's something Connie said to convince me to see you more often. But you know Connie."

Yes, she did. More than once, the sweet and fiery woman

of the Triple C Ranch had made her intentions clear. She wanted "her boys" to settle down with good wives and make grandbabies for her to spoil. Her interest in getting Nate and Whitney together had never waned.

"Connie's a natural born matchmaker. She can't help herself." Whitney spread the paper napkin on her lap.

"Do you mind too much?" Nate stretched a hand to the middle of the table and turned his palm up in silent invitation. She linked her fingers with his. Warm. Solid. Strong and earthy. His hands described the man.

"I think it's kind of...sweet."

"You do? So, does that mean"—he kept his voice low so nearby diners couldn't overhear—"you'd consider being more than friendly neighbors?"

Did she dare? Would she be making another mistake?

Whitney licked suddenly dry lips and swallowed. Time to get real. Kissing wasn't something she did casually. Not anymore. She liked this cowboy a lot. He'd been in her heart and mind for weeks. She might as well be honest about it.

Her gaze flicked up to his. She saw her uncertainty reflected in his eyes. He was scared too. Scared but willing to take the risk. For her.

The realization bolstered her courage. "I'd like that. A lot."

Nate blew out a held breath. His thumb rubbed up and down on her index finger. "I said I wouldn't do this again."

Whitney batted her eyes against the sudden wave of emotion. "Me too."

"I won't rush you," he promised softly. "We'll go slow, spend more time together."

She didn't know how *more time* was possible, but she wasn't complaining. She could never get enough of his company. Was she being stupid again? Risking not only herself but her daughters?

"No expectations, no demands."

"Okay," he said. "If that's how you want it."

She didn't. The reckless Whitney was an all-or-nothing kind of girl. But for now, that's how it had to be.

Their order arrived and she pulled her hand back. Conversation disappeared in the rustle of wax-paper-lined plastic baskets and the mouthwatering smells of real, home-made hamburgers and fresh-cut French fries.

Whitney cut up Sophia's mini-burger and added a dollop of ketchup to her basket. When she turned to do the same for Olivia, Nate was already there.

Like a father taking care of his daughter.

The action, so normal for most people, wasn't for Whitney. She and the twins had always been on their own. To have a friend, a partner, a man, show them such care soothed a bruised place inside.

No wonder she was falling in love with this Calypso cowboy.

And where was the caution in that?

That he wanted to take their relationship to the next level both elated and terrified her. Here was a man she believed she could trust, a man who cared about her daughters, a man who treated her with respect and tenderness.

A man who'd proved himself trustworthy.

If only she could trust herself.

The tornado of emotions swirled in her chest as she ate the best burger on the planet and talked to Nate about ordinary things. The pumpkin patch. The new goat kids. Her plans for the ranch and her excitement about the possibilities.

Nate told her about the Triple C's upcoming ranch rodeo —a fundraiser for cancer research—and she offered to help Emily and Connie with the concession and pie sale, or anywhere she was needed. Volunteering for the community fundraiser made her feel good, connected, a part of something bigger than herself.

Being with Nate made her feel good, too.

Under the surface of every exchange was the hint of romance. Little touches and quick glances that ended with secret smiles. They were more than friends. Maybe they had been for a while.

When the conversation turned to family, she listened to childhood tales of three ornery brothers and an adored baby sister. He spoke of his mother and dad, and she heard the pain of their loss in his words.

"What about *your* family, Whitney? Shouldn't you try to mend fences? If not for yourself, for the twins?"

She fiddled with a golden fry, dipping it in and out of ketchup without tasting.

"I've been gone from home since I was seventeen, Nate. I don't even know them anymore."

She still recalled the foolish nonsense she'd spouted to her parents. Their negativity was bringing her down. She was old enough to make her own choices. As they'd predicted, she'd brought herself down. In her rebellion, she'd lost them and everything else.

"That was in the past. What about now?"

"I don't know. They won't talk to me."

"When's the last time you tried?"

She stuck the fry in her mouth and chewed to delay answering. Finally, she admitted, "When I was pregnant with the twins."

"Nearly three years? That's a long time." He aimed a fry at her. "If they're decent people—and since they raised you, I'm guessing they are—you need to make contact, work out your differences."

Pride rose in her chest, tight, painful. "Too much bad water under the bridge."

"Have you prayed about it?"

With a shake of her head, Whitney reached for another fry buried deep within a glob of ketchup. The oversaturated potato wobbled like a noodle. "They said a lot of hurtful things."

"And you didn't?"

"You don't understand." Her great day was going south in a hurry. She crammed the soggy French fry into her mouth and chewed.

"I don't want to get preachy on you, Whit, but when we have issues with other people, we have to try to fix them. As Christians, it's on us to do the right thing even when it's hard." He fiddled with his straw, his focus on her. "Family's important. You won't regret trying."

Ketchup tangy on her tongue, Whitney considered his advice. In the time since the twins' birth, since she'd met Jesus, she'd thought about her family a lot. Had they forgiven her? Could they ever? Had she done everything in her power to make amends?

Of course she wanted her family back in her life. The twins deserved to know their grandparents, and the mother and dad she remembered from childhood, before she'd rebelled and gone wild, were great.

While they finished their burgers, she mulled the situation and listened as Nate greeted other customers. She heard so many new names, she'd never keep them straight.

The Burger Barn was crowded. Normal, Nate claimed, especially on a Saturday. Chatter was loud and chairs scraped the concrete floor. Over everything were Aunt Mint's robust greetings and the fragrant scent of grilled burgers.

Whitney could see herself staying in this small, friendly town forever. She'd been searching for home for a long, long time, and she'd finally found it.

Around the crowded café, she saw farmers with their farmers' tans, ranchers in their cowboy hats, moms and dads with their little ones, and teenagers paired-up and moony-eyed.

At the register, Aunt Mint talked to a man in a blue shirt who looked faintly familiar. Whitney squinted, trying to place him. As he turned to leave, she blinked. Once. Twice.

Was that Ronnie Flood, her very distant cousin? And if it was, what was he doing in Calypso?

Nate carried a sleeping Olivia to the front porch while Whitney dug for keys and pushed open the door. She held the screen with her back to let him enter first. He shot her a glance and winked as he stepped inside. As much as he liked playing daddy to the little girls, right now he was interested in some alone time with their mom.

"Put her in the crib," Whitney said. "I'll change her into pajamas later."

She turned and started back down the single step toward his truck, long hair swinging around her shoulders. That red hair enthralled him, like the rest of her.

"I'll get Sophia in a minute," he called after her.

Whitney waved a hand over one shoulder and went right on walking. Stubborn woman, accustomed to being on her own. She had trouble letting him help her with anything except the ranch, and once she mastered a skill, she elbowed him out of the way and got down to it. No wonder her admired her. She was some kind of special.

Flipping the interior light switch with one free finger, he carried the dark-haired darling to her room, kissed her forehead, and settled her into the crib. As he removed her shoes, she murmured his name, and a well of emotion stirred under his ribcage such as he'd never expected to feel for someone else's child. He had minimal experience with kids, but the twins had caught him in their charming net and wrapped themselves firmly around his heart. Exactly like their mother.

And he didn't ever want to get loose.

Not that he was ready to share that particular piece of information with Whitney, but soon, he hoped. Soon, she'd know he was falling in love with her. Falling hard and fast.

Time and again, he'd reminded himself that she was not like Alicia. Whitney had known heartache, too. Every day his feelings grew, and, all the while, like some kind of Doppler radar homed in on a coming storm, his internal warning system beeped caution.

Today had been too wonderful for caution. He'd felt like a husband and a dad on an autumn outing with his beautiful family. When the woman at the pumpkin patch had assumed they were a family, he'd been thrilled.

A lump formed in his throat as he removed Olivia's shoes and jacket and gazed down at the little girl, so smart and spunky like her mama.

Whitney entered the room with Sophia in her arms. Tenderly, Nate took the child and settled her into the crib beside her sister.

"They're getting big," she murmured. "My little babies."

"They're outgrowing this crib for certain." Nate unzipped the Velcro on Sophia's shoes, gently tugged them off, and handed them to Whitney. They were barely as big as his palm.

"I know." She took the tiny gray-and-pink sneakers and lined them up on top of a dresser that could use a coat of paint. Sally's, he supposed. "They need separate toddler beds, but those will have to wait until next year."

A cloud passed through his sunshiny thoughts.

Next year, she'd said. Until the inheritance was settled. Until she sold the ranch and moved on. The woman confused him. Big plans for the ranch one minute. Talk of leaving in a year in the next.

With two fingers, he rubbed the spot in the center of his chest that suddenly ached like a blend of heartburn and heartache. He'd said he wouldn't do this again, but here he was, running full out toward disaster. Unlike the disaster with Alicia, he could see this one coming, and he still couldn't stop himself.

"Nate?"

He turned toward her, aware that he'd been staring down at her beautiful daughters while his mind had filled with conflict. None of that was her problem. She'd been straight with him from the beginning. The decision to be with her was his, whatever the cost.

"A couple of treasures you've got here, Ms Brookes," he said, keeping things light, though his heart felt heavy.

"I know," she whispered. "Oh, Nate, I know. Every day I thank God for the gift of these two girls and pray He keeps them safe and well."

Her declaration moved him. She tried so hard in everything she did, but mothering was who she was. He wanted to promise to keep the twins safe, to keep her safe, always. To be there for her, for all of them.

How could he do that if she left next year? Or any year after?

Whitney flipped on a ladybug nightlight and moved toward the doorway to turn off the overhead lighting. She stood in the dim nursery, backlit from the living room, a golden glow around her.

He couldn't resist. He stepped close, his boot-toes touching the tips of the old tennis shoes she'd worn on their outing. The girls had nice shoes. She didn't. And that touched him too.

This woman got to him in more ways than he could count.

He didn't want her to go. Ever. She needed him. He needed her.

A pulse throbbed in his neck. If he said anything, he might scare her away sooner rather than later. But he had to know. He had to understand. It was the only way to be prepared when the ax fell.

"Why all the big plans?"

Whitney tilted her head. "What do you mean?"

"Today." His voice was shaky. He cleared his throat. "We made plans for the farm. Good plans. Long-term plans. Why bother if you're not going to stay here?"

She blinked. Twice. "Who said anything about leaving?"

"You did. After the year. After you gain ownership of the farm. You'll sell out and move on."

"I never said that." She placed a hand on his chest. She could probably feel his heart racing. "The ranch is my home now. A place for my girls. I want to build it up and make it successful."

Had he misread her? Misunderstood? He was good at misreading people.

Hope pushed up, lingered. "That'll take more than a year."

"Yes, it will, and I'm okay with that."

His heart gave one hard thump. "So, you're staying?"

"Yes, of course, I'm staying. I love this place."

Relief seeped in like flood waters and brought with it joy. She didn't plan to sell the ranch.

He'd never been so glad to be wrong in his entire life.

She was a breath away, her warmth emanating across the space to draw him closer.

He slid his hands over hers and up her arms, resting them on her red silken hair, mussed from the wind and activity but no less mesmerizing. Neither of them spoke, but his mind chanted, *she's staying, she's staying.*

His heart music tuned up, a symphony.

When he moved his fingers—calloused as they were—gently up her soft neck and over her velvet jaw, she shivered.

"Sorry." He let his hands drop, though his voice remained a low throb of sound in the quiet room. "A cowboy's hands are too rough."

With a soft, mysterious smile, she tugged his fingers back to her face. "I like your touch. Manly. Strong."

Pleasure jolted through him, electric.

Slowly he outlined the curves of her face, memorizing the texture of her skin.

With a near reverence, he traced her jaw, her eyebrows, and finally her lips. Her breath was soft against his skin, sending a tremor through him.

Beneath his fingers, her mouth curved.

"That tickles," she whispered, "in a really good way."

Her hands were on him now, light as a downy feather,

copying his moves, investigating the firm angles of his jaw, the rough five o'clock shadow, before settling on his lips.

"You're right," he murmured. "That tickles."

With a soft laugh, enjoying their romantic game, he nipped her finger, and she yelped, laughing to let him know she wasn't hurt. She liked the game too.

Behind him, one of the babies stirred, sighed, and settled again. Hands cupping her face, Nate backed Whitney into the narrow hallway and pulled the door closed behind him.

Then, before he exploded into a million pieces, Nate guided her against the wall and let his tickled lips do the talking.

AFTER NATE'S DEPARTURE, Whitney relived the romantic encounter as she practically floated to the twin's room. She still couldn't imagine where he'd gotten the crazy idea that she wanted to sell the ranch, but one thing for sure, when he'd discovered the truth, he'd seemed delighted, relieved.

He cared for her. Really cared.

She stood at the crib and looked at her babies the way she'd seen Nate doing. Her girls idolized the man, and, from all appearances, he'd fallen under their spell.

And she had fallen under his.

She brushed wild black hair away from Sophia's face and repeated the loving gesture with Olivia. Her treasures, he'd called them, and he was right. Even if she owned nothing, she would be rich.

Olivia hiked her bottom into the air and curled her hands beneath her. Accustomed to her sister's restlessness, Sophia never moved.

The girls had exhausted themselves at the pumpkin patch, and now they slept so soundly, she didn't bother to undress them any further. They would survive a night in purple sweat pants and T-shirts.

She left the room, her mind filled with two things—Nate and her parents. He was right. She had to try again to set things right. She wanted to. She needed to. The twins deserved no less. Nate had given her the push she needed to get moving.

She took the cell phone from her jeans' pocket and stared at the screen. Was their number the same? Did they even have a landline anymore?

Suddenly nervous and doubting herself, she wandered into the bedroom, kicked off her tennis shoes, and sat back against the hard oak headboard. Her pulse fluttered in her throat.

She was scared. Terrified, really. Would they hang up? Reject her? Remind her again that she'd made her bed and now she had to sleep in it?

Ugly arguments of the past flashed through her head until her courage began to flag. Maybe tomorrow morning would be a better time to call.

She started to put the phone away, but a sentence fluttered through her mind. *God has not given us a spirit of fear but of power and of love...*

During a time when Whitney had been so afraid of the future, a counselor at the pregnancy center had given her a card imprinted with those powerful words. That Bible verse had carried her through.

"God has not given me a spirit of fear," she repeated.

Eyes closed, she drew in a slow, calming breath and

prayed for courage and strength to cover the next few minutes and for the loving words to speak.

"Help me do this right."

Then she pushed in the phone number and waited.

THIRTY MINUTES LATER, Whitney fell to her knees beside the bed and prayed again. This time a prayer of thanksgiving.

She'd begun the call in repentance, asking for nothing but their forgiveness, proclaiming her love, proclaiming her sorrow at losing the best parents in the world, and sharing the news of her perfect twin girls and God's blessing through Sally Rogers's will.

Slowly, her mother had warmed to the conversation. By the end of the call, they were both in happy tears. Best of all, Mom and Dad wanted to meet the twins and had invited her to come home for Thanksgiving.

When the sobs of relief finally ended, Whitney rose to her feet and, smiling through tears, pushed in Nate's number.

"I know it's late," she said as soon as his warm baritone sounded in her ear.

"Never too late for you. Especially if you called to tell me I'm awesome and you had a great time today."

Heart soaring, she laughed. "You are and I did, but that's not why I called."

"No? What's up?"

"I called my parents."

"Good for you. And it went well, didn't it? I hear the joy in your voice."

"Yes. They want to visit me soon and meet the twins, and they invited us home for Thanksgiving."

"You're going?"

"If my budget allows."

"You're going. End of subject."

"Okay." She sniffled. "Oh, Nate, I'm so happy. They want me back. They missed me too but they didn't know how to find me. Thank you for giving me the courage to call."

"No credit here. God is good."

"So good. I prayed and stepped out on faith and look what happened."

He chuckled, a sound that tickled her ear and her heart. "Will you be able to sleep at all tonight?"

"I don't know. My pulse is racing with excitement."

"Adrenaline high." He yawned. "Sorry."

"No need to apologize. I'll let you go. I thought you'd want to know."

"You thought right. I wish I didn't require sleep. I miss you already."

"See you in the morning?"

"You can count on it. Goodnight, sweetheart."

"'Night, Nate."

She'd no more than clicked the end tab than a message light blinked on the screen. It was Nate.

Whitney grinned as she opened the text.

"Sweet dreams. I love you."

If she'd been happy before, she was now ecstatic.

She texted back, "I love you too," and then pressed the phone to her chest, filled.

Could life get any better?

TOO EXCITED TO SLEEP, she showered and relived the conversations with her parents and Nate. Then, after a peek at the sleeping twins, Whitney headed outside to the mailbox. Darkness lay over the land with no moon above, but the security light illuminated her walk to the end of the driveway and the rural mailbox.

Most days, she received *occupant* junk mail and Sally's catalogs, but utilities were due, and she was also still paying off credit card debt, a desperate choice during a desperate time. If Nate knew how many debtors chased her, he'd jump on Uncle Buck and ride into the sunset, just like in the movies.

No, that wasn't true. He wouldn't. Nate wasn't the running kind. Nor was he the cheating kind. He'd said he loved her, and she believed him. Everything in his actions said he did.

She'd read his text over and over again, and it still read the same. A fine, upstanding man like Nate Caldwell loved her, a woman who'd messed up most everything in her life for the last ten years.

She sighed and touched her mouth. Her cowboy's kisses were better than any romance movie she'd ever watched. Passionate and hot, tender and loving, he stirred her blood, but even more, he stirred her heart and soothed that damaged place deep inside that yearned to be cherished.

Billy, the silly goat, spotted her shadow moving down the driveway and let out a *baa* followed by a slam of his head into the metal fence. She spun around to be sure he couldn't get out, but all the gates within sight were safely secured. She squinted toward the barn. Though she could only see it in shadowy relief, everything appeared normal. If someone was playing tricks on her, they hadn't stopped by today while she was gone.

Shaking off the worry, she tried again to convince herself

that the incidents and mishaps were her own fault. No one was playing tricks. As the sheriff had reminded her, she was a newbie rancher. Things got spilled. Doors and gates got left open. The more she learned from Nate, the fewer mistakes she'd make.

But Nate had been worried, too, though neither of them had mentioned the incidents or the fire in a while. Things had settled down. Everything was safe and secure. Life was good.

A stillness lay across the land as the chilly fog of autumn moved in. Tree shadows streaked dark fingers over the barn and chicken house where all was peaceful. The birds had gone inside to roost. Even Mick Jagger would be mercifully silent until morning.

She'd come so far in such a short time. Thanks to the Lord Jesus, who'd blessed her with this place and with a real man to love.

The lawn was mowed and tidy, and the potholed driveway smoothed. On either side of the porch, a flower bed had been created and outlined with railroad ties, ready to burst into bloom next spring. The lawn and driveway were Nate's doing, the flower beds hers and Connie's. Hay was stacked in the barn loft for winter, stalls and shelters lined with fresh straw. On the front porch, colorful chalk drawings, barely discernible beneath the porch light, evoked a smile. Her babies. Her daughters. Her loves and her life.

Whitney strolled to the mailbox, reveling in the new contentment. She credited Nate with so much, although she was content within herself too, and that feeling had been a long time coming.

Failure after failure, mistake after mistake, but those

were behind her now, covered by the redemptive love of Jesus.

Metal squeaked against metal as she opened the mailbox and retrieved a small stack of envelopes.

Back inside the house, she tossed the stack on the table and poured a glass of ice water from the fridge, humming the twin's favorite song. "This little light of mine, I'm gonna let it shine."

Happy. Fulfilled. Content. In love.

She flipped through the envelopes, tossing out the junk, until she came to a letter without an address. Only her first name, in bold type, appeared on the plain white envelope.

"That's strange." Frowning, curious, she broke the seal and pulled out a single typewritten page.

You and your daughters are in danger. Leave now while you can. Say nothing to Caldwell, or both of you will pay the price. Ranch accidents are real killers, and fire danger is still high. You and Caldwell were lucky the first time. You won't be again. If that's not enough to convince you to leave Calypso, just remember: children are easy prey. Keep your mouth shut and leave. And don't come back.

A cry rose in Whitney's chest and jammed in her throat. She clapped a hand over her mouth to hold in the terrified sound. Every hair on her body stood up.

Somebody wanted to hurt her babies, and they'd hurt Nate, too.

But she couldn't leave. This was her home. This was all she had. Her children needed this ranch.

She read the note again, saw the innuendos. This person had set the fire that nearly burned the Triple C. Had it been meant for her? Or for them both?

Hands shaking so hard, she could hardly get her phone

from her back pocket, she punched nine and one before coming to her senses. She couldn't call the police. Even if Sheriff Hawk saw this note as proof, she had no idea who or where her enemy was, and she'd be putting her children and Nate in danger.

She wanted to call Nate. Oh, how she needed him, but the note threatened him, too.

Quaking, breathless, she rushed down the hall and looked in on the girls. They remained where she'd left them, undisturbed.

"Thank you, Father."

Blood rushing in her ears and knees wobbly, she raced from door to door and window to window to secure the house.

Then she dug out the baseball bat she kept stored in the closet—the one she'd never expected to need in Calypso—and sat down on the couch to pray and keep watch the rest of the night.

IN THE FOYER of Evangel Church, Nate went to the glass door and stared out at the crowded parking lot one more time. The service would start in a couple of minutes, and Whitney had yet to arrive. The only time she'd missed church since her arrival had been when one of the twins was sick. Even with two little ones to get ready, she was never late.

He frowned at the tree-lined street running parallel to the parking lot and willed the old Subaru to appear. He wanted to see her. Needed to be with her, especially after yesterday.

The fellowship streamed in, jostling and chatting the

way they always did in the entryway before church. The congregation wasn't large, and everyone knew everyone.

Visiting on Sunday mornings was a community event. Nate and Ace had done their share while waiting, and he was thankful to have his brother in church again after the last few bumpy years. But Ace wasn't his worry this morning. Whitney was.

Emily came out of the sanctuary, a bulletin in one hand. "Hey, guys, service is about to start. We're on the left side."

"Whitney's not here yet."

His sister's black eyebrows lifted. "Have you talked to her this morning?"

"She texted and told me not to come over. Said she'd take care of the animals herself." He'd thought the text was odd considering last night's conversation, but he hadn't questioned it. They kept chores minimal on Sunday. She was being thoughtful.

"Maybe her car finally gave up."

Nate frowned. He should have taken a look at the old Subaru, winterized it for her.

"When temperatures dip, old batteries can quit, old tires can go flat." Ace paused to greet a friend, his grin flashing, before he looked back at Nate. "Call her."

"Yes, worry wart. Call her." Emily put a hand on his shoulder. "Your heart is showing."

Nate didn't care if it was.

"If she's running late and in the middle of dressing the girls, she has her hands full. I'll text." His fingers flew over the message.

In seconds, her response appeared. Nate scowled at the phone. "She's not coming. Says she has things to do and she's too tired."

One of Ace's black eyebrows rose in sly speculative expression. "The two of you must have had a wild date last night."

Nate elbowed his brother. "Cut it out. You're in church."

Ace laughed. "Joking. But cut the lady some slack. With two kids and the ranch and now you to keep her busy, she has a right to be tired."

"I guess that's true. Yesterday was pretty exhausting for all of us. Good but tiring. And when we last spoke, she'd said she was too excited to sleep."

That was it. She hadn't slept much. Excitement over the talk with her parents had kept her awake.

While he and his brother had bottle-fed orphaned calves this morning, he'd told Ace of his feelings and that he and Whitney were moving things up a notch. Regardless of his teasing, Ace was supportive and encouraging. Everyone on the Triple C liked their spunky neighbor. The way she'd pulled her weight the night of the fire had won widespread approval, and nobody could miss her hard work on Sally's ranch. Correction. Whitney's ranch.

The strains of *Amazing Grace* floated out from the sanctuary.

Ace clapped a hand on his shoulder. "Time to go in. You can stop by Whitney's place later."

"Right." As long as she and the twins were okay, he could see them this afternoon. He didn't like spending the morning without them, but he would live.

During service, Nate struggled to keep his mind on the pastor's message. Something about Whitney's text bothered him. It had been abrupt, terse, as if she didn't want to talk to him.

Or maybe he was being paranoid. Meaning was hard to

discern in a text. Admittedly, he was on unsteady ground. He'd stuck his heart out again, and the fear of falling on his face was real. What if Whitney had changed her mind about him? What if she regretted their conversation and all those kisses and words of endearment the night before?

She was scared of making another mistake too. Had his declaration of love been too soon? Had he scared her away? He swallowed the knot of anxiety and refocused on the sermon.

After church, they'd talk. Everything would be fine.

But before service ended, he got a call from the sheriff that dozens of cows had broken fence and were out on a busy highway. By the time, he'd gathered the cows and moved them to another pasture, the day was done, and so was he. Before he fell into bed, he shot a text to Whitney. *Missed you today. See you tomorrow.* And once again he added, *Love, Nate.*

14

S unday night while she and her babies slept, someone raided the chicken pen, and three hens went missing. Another warning note was tacked inside the barn door. The typed print sent the message loud and clear.

Leave before someone dies.

Chest hurting so badly, she wondered if a woman her age could have a heart attack, Whitney texted Nate and told him not to come over because she had business in town. Unlike his sweet text from last night, she didn't add her love. He had to believe she'd had second thoughts. That was the only way. Otherwise, he'd do something crazy and get himself hurt.

After locking the twins inside the house, she made the rounds, caring for the animals, tears falling with every butt from the goats and cackle from her comical hens. When ornery Clive snuggled under her arm, she fought back a sob. By the time, she got to the new baby goats, she had to sit down in the stall, hug them to her, and weep.

Back inside the house, she tried to hide her heartache from the twins, but they saw her tears and reacted with worry.

"Mama, don't cry. 'Livia loves you." Tiny arms wrapped around her leg as the baby repeated the phrase Whitney said to her girls any time they got upset. Their compassion and kindness only made the tears fall more freely.

"Sophia, too." Sophia patted her own chest. "I, Mama. I."

Olivia tilted her face upward, expression tender and worried. "Did you got a boo-boo?"

Whitney went to her knees and held the girls tightly against her. Sophia patted her back.

Stiffening her resolve with a reminder that the girls were in danger, she sniffed back the tears. "No, baby. Mama's tired this morning. That's all."

Tired of life kicking her in the teeth.

Someone wanted her to fail, and now she was convinced the man she'd seen in the Burger Barn *was* the other heir to Sally's ranch—Ronnie Flood. Ronnie was the only one who stood to gain if she walked away from this ranch and Calypso.

She had no idea what kind of man he was, but anyone who would threaten innocent children must be a horrible excuse for a human being. He shouldn't be allowed to get away with this. There had to be something she could do to stop him.

She considered the choices. Involve Nate and risk his life. Tell the sheriff and risk her children as well as Nate. Neither was a choice she could live with. Any man who would intentionally set the fire that had nearly burned the Triple C was evil enough to do worse. She could feel it deep in her gut. They were all in danger.

Her only viable option was St. Louis. Go home. To her parents. Where the girls would be safe.

Leaving the ranch meant losing it forever, but what else could she do? Her daughters and Nate were worth more than this ranch. More than anything.

"God has not given me the spirit of fear," she muttered. But if that was true, why were her hands shaking? Why was she about to run away?

She needed advice and she needed it bad, and the only other person who would understand was her lawyer.

Gritty eyed and muzzy-headed from fatigue, she drove into Calypso. The blue sky and fall foliage, usually a favorite, were lost on her, as was the upbeat music pumping from her radio. She clicked it off. She tried to pray, but her thoughts jumbled and spun, making no sense even to her. God must think she was a real loser.

Running on adrenaline, fear, and a full pot of strong coffee, Whitney scanned the street in front of the law offices of Harold and Leach. Monday morning traffic puttered along the main streets, and car doors slammed as the work week reconvened. A well-dressed woman toting a disposable coffee cup stepped up on the curb next to her and smiled before going inside the bank.

In the crisp autumn breeze, Calypso appeared perfectly normal, perfectly safe. If Ronnie was watching, and he must be to know about her relationship with Nate, he was too smart to show himself.

The idea that he might be lurking nearby at this very moment scared her silly. Shielding the twins with her body, she gripped their hands and cast one last anxious look around before scurrying inside the law office.

A well-groomed receptionist with short, coiffed hair and red earrings removed her reading glasses. "May I help you?"

"I'd like to speak with Mr. Leach, please." Her voice trembled. She cleared her throat.

Don't panic. Do what you must.

"Do you have an appointment?"

"No, but tell him Whitney Brookes is here and it's urgent."

A professional smile creased the woman's face. "Have a seat. I'll see if he's available."

While she waited, Whitney jostled a twin on each knee and prayed. Sweat gathered on the back of her neck. Every tick of the clock hanging over the receptionist's desk made her jump.

She prayed the lawyer would use his expertise to protect her and the Caldwells. Maybe he could find Ronnie and confront him, threaten him with jail or a lawsuit. Attorneys knew how to do that sort of thing, didn't they?

But she had no idea where Ronnie was or what he was up to. Worse, he had given her no deadline. As long as she lived on the ranch, her children remained in danger. What if he did something diabolical to her car and it exploded? What if he was, even now, lying in wait at the ranch?

She started to shake again.

As tired as she was, the children were equally well-rested. They squirmed and whined to get down and play, and she was about to cave when the other woman returned.

"Mr. Leach can spare a few minutes for you. Go on back."

The walk down the hall to a door marked, *Arnold Leach, Attorney at Law,* was long and nerve wracking. Her stomach rolled and she had the awful notion that she might lose three cups of coffee on the gray Berber carpet.

"Whitney." Mr. Leach stood behind his desk, smiling like an old friend as he adjusted his suit coat. "Come in, my dear, and bring those darling children."

Whitney wobbled inside, closing the door behind her. She had a vague notion of elegant, sedate décor in shades of gray, but other than the client chairs that faced the desk, she couldn't have cared less. Without waiting to asked, she collapsed onto one of the seats and pulled the twins onto her lap.

Mr. Leach watched her with interest as he settled into his fancy leather chair. "You seem a bit discomposed this morning, Whitney. Is there something I can help you with? Problems with the inheritance or running the ranch? I do hope you haven't already gone through all of Sally's funds."

Olivia arched her back. "Down, Mommy. I want down now."

The girls were usually great when she took them out in public. Why today of all days did Olivia have to act up? Was she responding to the turmoil churning inside her mother?

Mr. Leach lifted his telephone receiver. "Perhaps my receptionist could watch your children while we talk."

"No!" The reply shot out with enough force to startle Olivia into submission. Whitney had startled herself. But she was not letting the twins out of her sight for a minute.

She sucked in a calming, though shaky breath. "They can be a handful sometimes. I prefer to keep them with me."

"As you wish." He put the phone down but his lips thinned in disapproval. He probably thought she was a terrible mother. "I have another client soon. So if there is something important we need to discuss...."

The lawyer let the sentence soak in. Whitney got the message. Speak her peace or get out.

"Someone is threatening my family and Nate Caldwell."

His bushy eyebrows jacked up into his receding hairline. "I beg your pardon?"

She told him about the notes and the strange incidents. "The incidents weren't because I'm an inept city girl. Someone was intentionally trying to sabotage my efforts so they could steal my inheritance."

"Who are on earth would do such a thing?"

"Ronnie Flood. Sally's back-up heir. The one you told me about that was raring to take over if I didn't want the ranch."

"Have you spoken to the man?"

"No, but I saw him at the Burger Barn on Saturday."

"Really?"

Didn't he believe her? "Mr. Leach, please. You're the only one I can talk to about this. I'm in danger. My girls are in danger. If Ronnie is to blame, he's also the one who set the fire that nearly burned out the Caldwell's ranch. He's dangerous, a threat to me and my girls."

The lawyer leaned forward. "Have you called the sheriff?"

"Not yet." She bit her lip. Did she sound like a hysterical nut? "Like you, he thought I was probably causing my own problems. Besides, according to the note, if I call the police, this note-writing maniac will do something terrible."

"So you haven't called?"

"No, of course not!"

"May I see this note? You did bring it with you, didn't you?"

She tugged the paper from her pocket and handed it

across the desk. His scowl deepened as he pursued the message.

"This is serious, indeed. I understand your concern. A call to the sheriff could have deadly repercussions."

The word *deadly* shot terror through her body. "I don't know what to do."

The man sat back in his black executive chair and stroked his chin, contemplating first her and then the note. Finally, he spoke.

"You did the right thing by coming to me with this. As your lawyer, I am deeply concerned for your well being and that of your little girls." He shot a hang-dog glance at the twins. "Such precious children, a gift from above. We must protect them at all costs."

"I agree completely. They're my life. I cannot let anything happen to them."

"Then, my dear girl, for their sakes, the solution is clear."

Whitney batted her eyes, baffled. "It is?"

"You must take them far away, some place where this Ronnie person or whomever is the culprit, can't find you. Move back to St. Louis, close to your family, where you and your children will be well protected."

"You know the conditions of the will. Mr. Leach, if I abandon the ranch, I lose it. Can't you find Ronnie and do something to stop him?"

"Investigations take time, my dear. As much as I'd like to resolve this differently, I fear you have little choice. As your attorney, I am advising you to return to your family in St. Louis immediately."

"But—"

The attorney folded his arms on the desk and leaned

forward, tone ominous. "Are you willing to risk your daughters for a ranch you didn't know existed a few months ago?"

When put like that, the answer was simple. In a whisper, she replied, "No."

He nodded, leaning back again. "Then trust me. Relinquishing that little ranch is absolutely the right choice. A novice such as yourself would never be able to make a living there anyway."

Whitney licked dry lips. Something about this felt all wrong, but she was so tired and scared, she couldn't think straight. She needed Nate. She needed to hear his advice and wisdom. But she didn't dare.

Mr. Leach shot her a professionally sympathetic glance. "Not everyone is cut out for the country life, and of course, you want to do what is best for your children. I will have my secretary prepare the proper paper work for your signature. Then all will be well."

Well? To leave everything she'd worked so hard for? To leave Calypso and Nate and her livelihood? She loved learning to be a rancher. She loved introducing her girls to the small animals and seeing them thrive in the healthy outdoors.

She also loved them too much to take the risk.

While she rung her hands, uncertain but out of good options, the lawyer lifted the telephone and spoke to someone. His secretary, Whitney supposed, because in minutes, a stick thin woman in bright blue pumps entered with a manila folder.

As Mr. Leach took it, his lips stretched in a thin smile. "Thank you, Patrice."

Patrice nodded and sailed out, shutting the door behind her. The click sounded like a gunshot to Whitney.

Whitney stared at the folder, aware she was about to give up a dream.

Was Mr. Leach correct? Was this really the only solution? Or was she making another colossal mistake?

Whitney's breath grew short until she feared she'd pass out. Her ears began to buzz, a dozen bees inside her head.

Leave before someone dies.

The message flashed through her mind and scared her senseless all over again. She had no choice. She had to do this.

Mr. Leach pulled a legal-looking sheet from the folder. "Here's all we need to protect your daughters from this hoodlum. Simply sign on the bottom line, Patrice will notarize, and you'll be free of that troublesome ranch."

Troublesome? Yes, but wonderful too. Those cute little creatures had saved her life. They'd given her a home. They'd brought her to Nate.

Tears burned the back of her nose. She sniffed them away. Don't think about the ranch. Think of Nate and Olivia and Sophia. For them. Just sign the paper.

Mr. Leach turned the sheet in her direction and slid it across the desk. Sweat had beaded on his forehead. Was he that afraid for her? Did he know something horrible about Ronnie that she didn't?

With trembling hand, she took the pen he offered. Her vision blurred as she tried to read over the legal document. She was so tired. Exhausted. Sleep-deprived. It was hard to know if this was the right thing to do.

"Me, Mommy. I write." Olivia grabbed for the pen. The movement jarred a long streak of ink down the page.

"Olivia!" Whitney appealed to the lawyer. "I'm sorry. Will this need to be retyped?"

Mr. Leach's face mottled. His eyes bulged. He looked anything but pleased. "You should have left the children with Patrice. Let me see the paper."

Whitney pushed the document his way and waited, embarrassed as he glared at the damage.

"I'm really sorry, Mr. Leach. The girls aren't accustomed to sitting still so long."

His mouth in a thin line, the attorney shoved the form in her direction. "Just sign it."

Surprised by his harsh tone, Whitney bristled. Why was he being so pushy and rude? She'd done nothing wrong.

Suddenly, her mind cleared and her spine straightened. God had sent her this ranch. Calypso was her home now. Her life was here. She had plans for the ranch, plans for her future. She loved her miniature animals, her new friends, her church, and Calypso. Most of all, she loved Nate Caldwell. There had to be something else she can do.

"I should think about this more. I'll let you know." She grabbed the paper along with her daughters' hands and hurried for the door.

"You're risking a great deal, my dear." His voice sounded ominous.

She spun around.

The attorney glared at her. "I hope you know what you're doing."

She had no idea.

With fear crawling down her back like black-widow spiders, she marched out of the office, muttering under her breath. "God has not given me the spirit of fear. Oh, help me, Jesus."

NATE STARED GRIMLY at the downed barbed wire fence, his hands on his hips as he studied the reason for yesterday's mass exit of cattle onto a busy roadway.

"You thinking what I'm thinking?" Gilbert squatted on the burned grass and lifted one end of wire.

"This fence was cut. All five strands."

"Makes a man wonder about that fire." Gilbert tossed the wire aside in disgust. "Was it intentional too?"

He'd been thinking the same thing for a long time. "But why? Who would cut our fence and let fifty head of cattle out on the highway where they could cause an accident?"

"We've never had any trouble before." Gilbert dusted his hands on his pant legs, sending up a puff of dust and soot, leftovers of the fire. "You or Ace riled anybody lately?"

Nate removed his hat and wiped a hand across his forehead. Though the day was cool, his mood was hot. "Not that I know of."

Not unless he counted Whitney, who had suddenly stopped communicating with him. She hadn't even answered his latest text.

Something was wrong.

He'd tried calling her after the odd "don't come over" text, but she hadn't picked up.

A bad feeling nagged at him. Had she changed her mind about him? About them? Was she trying to let him down easy?

He shouldn't have texted his love. Pretty dumb move. He should have told her in person. Was she upset about that? Or was she upset because he'd said it in the first place?

One thing he knew, after he'd laid his heart out on the line, Whitney had gone silent.

Even a dumb cowboy like him knew that was not a good sign.

"Cows aren't going to fix this fence," Gilbert said. "Might as well get to it."

Nate slapped his hat back on his head. He didn't want to work fence. He wanted to talk to Whitney, to clear things up, to be sure he hadn't blown his chance. But responsibility came before pleasure.

Together he and the foreman unloaded and settled in to the job.

"We should reinforce this road frontage all at once," Gilbert said as he unrolled a length of wire. "We brought plenty of supplies."

The last thing he wanted to hear. More work. A longer day.

Nate plucked the top wire on the next section like a guitar string and watched it sag. Gilbert was right. As usual.

With a resigned sign, Nate said, "The posts are good but this wire is getting old and the fire stretched it pretty badly."

In an hour they'd worked their way along the fence line, repairing and replacing. All the while Nate's mind raced and his gut gnawed. If worrying about Whitney wasn't enough, he had his own property to worry about. Somebody had cut his fence and maybe set the fire that had destroyed acres of prime winter pasture.

Somebody had also messed with Whitney's livestock, too.

He had no real evidence of that except for the little annoying problems that kept popping up, but he'd watched Whitney with the animals. Even though she was green to ranching, she was conscientious. He didn't believe she could be responsible for that many mishaps.

But after the sheriff had come out and looked around, the problems had stopped. Either that, or Whitney wasn't sharing her trouble with him.

Wire in hand, he paused to stare off in the direction of her house.

If she was hiding problems, what else was she keeping from him? Why hadn't she returned his calls? Why had she blown him off this morning?

"You're kind of spacey today, son." Gilbert unwound a length of barbed wire and offered one end to Nate. "Fretting about who did this?"

"A little." Nate shook the cobwebs out, worked the wire around the T-post, and tied it off with his pliers. "I'm worried about Whitney."

"She sick?"

"Not that I know of. She had to go into town this morning. Told me not to come over."

Leaning his full body weight, he stretched the wire to the next post and held it in place while Gilbert applied the stretchers. The Triple C prided itself on excellent fences and very few cattle on the loose. Last night had been the exception. A major exception he didn't want to happen again. Cattle on a roadway were a huge liability.

"So what's the problem?"

He hadn't seen her since Saturday night. That was the problem. One of them.

"I've been going to Whitney's place every morning since we met, and suddenly she doesn't want me there. She didn't come to church yesterday either. Something's wrong."

Gilbert laughed, his dark face crinkling in humor. "Son, you've got it bad. Did you have a fight?"

"No. Just the opposite." They'd had a great time on

Saturday at the pumpkin patch, and the evening had gotten better and better, ending with the sweetest words anyone could say. Or text.

He yanked hard on the wire and stomped toward the next post. "I keep having flashbacks of Alicia walking out on me, and I wonder if Whitney will do the same."

Gilbert sobered. "Stands to reason you'd be gun-shy after what Alicia did, but Whitney's different."

"I thought so too, but..."

"I can work on this." Gilbert nudged his chin toward the end of the fence row. "Go on over and talk to her. If she's not there, wait 'til she is."

Though Nate appreciated his friend's words, the ranch was his responsibility. "I finish what I start."

But as soon as they reached the end, he was out of here.

15

W hitney barricaded herself and the twins inside the ranch house and walked the floor, praying like a mad woman.

The only answer she heard was inside her head and her heart. *Tell Nate* was not a reasonable answer, no matter how much she wanted to do exactly that. The stakes were too high.

Yet, goodbye was the cruelest word in the English language. Could she do *that* to him? To herself and these girls who'd come to love him so much? Especially after she'd promised to stay in Calypso?

She walked through the little farmhouse that had become home, a real home filled with warmth and love. Over the weeks and months, she'd added a few touches here and there. Framed pictures of the twins, an ivy plant from Connie, a throw rug for the girls to play on, two bright print accent pillows from Emily. Next to Sally's dated couch, Nate and Gilbert had placed a pair of little rocking chairs for Olivia and Sophia. Early Christmas gifts, they'd said.

The thought of that sweet gesture brought tears.

She tipped the little chairs and watched them rock, imagining the twins there with their baby dolls as they watched *Peppa Pig*. Going to the window, she gazed out at the ranch in golden autumn and soaked up more things she loved about this place.

The big oak in the front yard had turned a deep red-orange, and squirrels raced each other for the acorns underneath. Out in the pens, the animals looked healthy and well prepared for winter.

Yes, she and the twins had thrived here. She'd grown as a mother, as a woman. Here in Calypso, she'd proven to herself that she was capable and strong, no longer a quitter who ran when life got too hard.

Was that what she was doing now? Running away again?

Giving in and giving up didn't seem right.

She rubbed a hand over her tight forehead and closed the door, anxious about who might be hiding in the barn or lurking in her fields.

Her fields.

Her cell phone vibrated against her hip. She didn't have to look to know the caller was Nate. He'd texted and phoned off and on all day. She didn't know what to say, so she hadn't replied. Not once. And she wouldn't now. Not until she knew for certain what to do.

Footsteps sounded outside on the porch. Fear shot up her spine. She spun toward the door and back again. Where were the girls?

"Olivia! Sophia!" She raced down the hall and found the twins in the nursery exactly where she'd left them, playing dress-up. Feet stuck inside Whitney's rubber boots and a baseball cap falling down over her ears, Sophia was assisting her twin into a tattered old jacket.

They were safe. They were okay. For now. But she couldn't live like this, worrying every second that someone would hurt them.

Breathing deeply to settle her adrenaline, baseball bat in hand, she squinted through the front door peep hole.

Her heart soared as her stomach fell. Nate stood on her porch.

He knocked again and, steeling her emotions, she put the bat against the wall and opened the door.

Nate held a bouquet of roses. Yellow.

"Hey." He said through the glass.

"Hi."

"Everything okay?"

How did she answer that?

Pushing the door open, she said, "You brought flowers."

A grin inched up his face, and Whitney wanted to hug him so badly, to be held in his arms and forget all about the terrifying notes and the paper she probably should have signed.

He stepped inside, bringing a clean, freshly showered smell and the hint of some woodsy cologne. Instead of his usual work attire, he'd dressed in pressed jeans and a light blue Cinch shirt she'd never seen before. Even his Sunday boots were polished to a brown sheen.

He'd dressed up for her. He'd brought her roses. This gentle cowboy she loved so much.

But if she loved him, wouldn't she do everything she could to protect him?

The confused voice in her head wouldn't hush. *Tell him. Tell him,* it said.

Her eyes dropped shut. *Oh, Lord, I don't know what to do.*

To cover her confusion, she buried her nose in the flowers and sniffed. "I love yellow roses."

"I know."

Of course he did. Just as she knew he liked picante sauce on everything, even his steak, and that he'd broken his arm jumping out of the barn loft when he was eight. And though he'd have made a great vet, he'd never resented coming home for good when his father died.

In return, she'd told him tales of growing up in the suburbs, of her insurance-salesman father and paralegal mother, of the plays she'd been in and the Spanish teacher she'd had a crush on. She'd even told him of time she'd thrown up on her desk in second grade.

They'd had too little time together and yet, it seemed as if they'd known each other forever.

Nate pushed the roses aside and leaned in for a kiss. Aching inside, afraid for him, and so unsure, she kissed him back, the taste bittersweet as he pulled her close. Whitney leaned into his chest, savoring the moment and the memory in case she had to walk away.

"I've wanted to do that all day," he murmured against her ear.

The man was killing her.

Slowly, she eased away from his solid comfort to memorize his wonderful, rugged face. She gulped back the tidal wave of emotion pressing, pressing against her eyelids.

"Whitney?" A crease appeared between his eyes as his expression shifted from affection to concern. "What's wrong? You look like your puppy got run over."

She licked her lips, tasting him there. "We need to talk."

But what would she say? The truth? Or a lie to protect him?

"I suspected something was wrong." He shifted his stance, wary now. "I'm listening."

Tears threatened. She batted her eyes against the impending flow.

"The flowers," she said quickly.

To hide the tears and her terrible, terrible worry, she hurried into the kitchen. Once there, she floundered. She didn't own a vase and if Sally did, she'd never seen it.

Not that a vase mattered at this moment.

Roses in hand, she stood at the sink, staring out the kitchen window. Was someone out there even now, aware she was here with Nate?

"Whit?" Nate followed, stopping at the scarred little table. "What's going on?"

"I—I" Slowly, she turned to face him, the roses forgotten.

Her heart stuttered. Nate stared down at the paper she'd left on the table. The paper Lawyer Leach had advised her to sign.

"Help me out here. What's happening?" He picked up the document. "What is this?"

"I think I should give up the ranch and go back to St. Louis."

"You what? What are you talking about?" His face grew incredulous. "That's crazy. You can't. You said..."

She waved a limp hand. "I think it's for the best."

"Best for who?"

"You. Me. The twins."

He stepped closer. She backed away.

"You're not making sense," he said. "Two nights ago, we made plans. You said you liked it here."

"I do. I love this ranch. I love Calypso." And you.

She pressed shaky fingers to her big mouth. She'd said too much.

Nate raised his hands in a timeout sign. "Whoa. Now, you're making even less sense. You love it here, but you're going back to St. Louis." He shook his head. "No sense at all. Two days ago, you said you loved—"

He put clenched fists on his hips and glanced to the side. The hurt in his brown eyes nearly took her to the floor. "I caused this, didn't I? You're leaving because of me. Because I spoke too soon, pushed our relationship too far too fast."

"No. No!" Her fingers twisted against her T-shirt. She was hurting him when she only wanted to protect him. "That's not true."

Those honest brown eyes came back to her and held on, seeking to understand, seeking the truth.

"Then talk to me, Whit," he said softly, voice aching. "Please. You're killing me. Explain what this is all about."

Everything in her yearned to do exactly that. But if she told him about the threats, was she risking his life? And that of her daughters?

The twins apparently had heard the voice of their hero and came stumbling into the room in their oversize play clothes. "Nate, Nate!"

Each girl grabbed one of his knees and wrapped her legs around his shin. It was a game they played. The twins latched on like baby monkeys and the strong cowboy walked them around the room, as stiff-legged as Frankenstein.

Now was not a good time. "Girls, go play. Leave Nate alone. Get down."

Three sets of brown eyes stared at her. One was so

confused, she had to look away. When Nate began to march the twins around the kitchen, the tears she'd kept inside trickled onto her cheeks.

The twins giggled and she cried. A headache throbbed behind her eyes.

Her baby girls needed this wonderful man who'd been a father to them. They needed his gentle roughness, his manly way of doing things. So did she.

While she watched, he walked them down the hall and through the nursery door. She heard the rumble of his voice and more giggles before he returned without them.

"You're crying." Nate touched his rough fingertips to her cheek. "I hate seeing you cry. Tell me what's wrong. If it's me, if I messed up, if you don't want me in your life, say so, and I'll go. But if you love this ranch, don't give it up. You've worked too hard."

The tears turned to a flood. Leave it to Nate to shoulder the blame and think of her. No wonder she loved him so much.

"I'm afraid."

"Me, too, darling. We've both been hurt." Completely misunderstanding her fear, his rancher's hands gently gripped her upper arms and drew her closer. "But with God's help—"

Whitney placed a hand on his chest to stop him. "That's not what I mean, Nate. He said he'll hurt you. He'll hurt my babies unless I sign over the ranch."

Nate stiffened. His fingers tightened against her arms.

With a steel fury in his voice she'd never heard before, he ground out, "Someone threatened you? Is that what this is about?"

The awful trembling returned. "I shouldn't have told you. Now something terrible will happen."

"Who was it?" His eyes narrowed. A cheek muscle twitched. "Give me a name."

"I don't know for sure. He left notes, one in the mailbox and another stuck on the barn door this morning."

"Show me."

Whitney retrieved the notes and watched, trembling, as Nate read each one. When he'd finished, the most dangerous expression she'd ever seen hardened his face.

"Nobody will ever hurt you or those babies. Not on my watch. This ends today."

16

The sheriff's SUV pulled in behind Nate's truck, and a uniformed Lawson Hawk stepped out and slammed the door. The sound echoed over the ranch. If anyone was watching her house, they'd know the sheriff was here.

Second thoughts peppered Whitney's mind as she stood beside Nate on the porch. Her knees turned to Jell-O. "He said not to call the police."

"We got this, babe. Be strong. You're not in this alone." Nate slipped a reassuring arm across her shoulders as they stepped out to meet the officer.

Nate's confidence strengthened her. She wasn't alone anymore. The concept was almost too foreign to receive.

Sheriff Hawk stepped up on the porch, equipment rattling against his side. His glaze flickered over the house, the yard, the animals. He even seemed to note Nate's arm around her shoulders before his gaze settled on her. Like the bird for which he was named, the sheriff was sharp-eyed, missing little.

"Sounds like you got trouble." He offered a hand.

Nate shook it. "Thanks for coming, Lawson. Like I told you on the phone, someone is threatening her and the twins."

Whitney looked up at her cowboy. If he wouldn't protect himself, she'd do it for him. "And you, too, Nate."

"Yeah, well." He shifted uncomfortably. "That's beside the point. It's you and the girls I worry about."

"So tell me what happened. Start at the beginning."

"Can we go inside the house?" she asked. "Please." The idea of standing in the open was too scary to consider. She wanted to barricade her babies in a safe room and stay there until this was over.

The men must have heard the fear in her voice because they followed her.

"I don't want to scare the twins." Nate perched on the edge of the sofa as if ready to move on a moment's notice. "Let's try to stay calm and keep our voices low."

"Let me look in on them first." Whitney hurried down the short hall, saw the girls engaged in animated play, and rushed back to where the two men were already deep in conversation. Nate grabbed her hand and tugged her down. His nearness calmed her, assured her that everything would be all right.

The sheriff turned his attention to her. He had a notebook on his lap and a pen in his hand. "Your turn, Whitney. Nate showed me the notes you found. One in the mailbox and one in the barn. Correct?"

"Yes, sir. Saturday night when I came home, I found the first one in the mailbox. Sunday morning the other was tacked to the barn."

"It's pretty clear now that the problems you were having

on the ranch weren't accidental."

Whitney shook her head, relieved that he believed her this time. "That's right."

The blue eyed sheriff gave her a long look. He must have seen the anxiety she couldn't shake. "You're safe now. Threats are just that, but this first note admits culpability to vandalism and arson. We'll get him. Start at the beginning. Tell me everything you remember that might have the slightest relevance."

So, voice shaking, and terrified Ronnie would somehow learn she'd told the police, Whitney shared her story. She told him about the will's requirements and the distant relative she only knew by sight, and about every incident on the ranch.

"You should have called me immediately." The sheriff's face was grim.

"That's what I told her."

"I was too afraid. I couldn't take the chance." She grappled for Nate's hand, fingers clammy in the fall air. "And my lawyer said I was doing the right thing, so I thought if I left town—"

"Your lawyer?" The sheriff leaned in, eyes narrowed. "He advised you not to contact the police?"

She nodded. "He was worried for my safety and for my twins. He gave me the paper to sign and said I should get my girls away from here as soon as possible."

The two men exchanged glances.

"Something about that doesn't sound right to me," Nate said. "What about you, sheriff?"

"I thought the same thing," Whitney said. "It just happened so fast, and I wasn't sure. That's why I didn't sign the papers even after he got upset."

Next to her, Nate's body tensed. "He was upset? Because you refused to sign away your inheritance?"

Lawson's contemplative look sharpened. "I think we should have a talk with your lawyer. What's his name?"

"Arnold Leach. He's the one who called me in the first place and told me about the inheritance. His office is on Old Main right across from the dollar store."

"I know where it is." Lawson scribbled something on his pad. "If nothing else, he's a link to this Ronnie Flood person. Leach might have contact information."

"Check him close, Lawson. I want to know why he'd insist she sign that paper."

"Will do." The two men exchanged telling looks.

Did they suspect her attorney? If not for Arnold Leach, she would never have known about the inheritance. He couldn't be involved. Yet, he'd been insistent, almost threatening, this morning. And hadn't he visited her ranch the morning the feed was first spilled and the goat escaped?

Now she was getting paranoid.

"Can she bunk over at your place for a few days while we find this guy?" the sheriff was saying.

Nate nodded as he rose with the other man. "I already have orders from Connie and Emily to bring her home. We'll put some men on round the clock guard duty. She'll be safe there."

"Good." To Whitney, Lawson said, "Pack a few things and go to the Triple C. We'll have you back in your house in no time."

As SHAKEN as he could ever remembering being, Nate followed Whitney's car to the Triple C. She'd been pale as paste, trembling like an earthquake, and he'd worried about her driving, but she'd insisted she was all right.

She wasn't all right. Neither was he. In fact, he vacillated between an anger hot enough to spark a forest fire and tenderness for a certain redhead strong enough to bring him to his knees. Whitney hadn't been trying to dump him. She'd been trying to protect him.

And he had every intention of returning the favor.

Connie met them as they parked in the circle drive alongside the steps of the big house. With a spate of Spanish and prayers and assurances that God was their fortress and strong tower, she helped Whitney unload the twins.

Nate believed in prayer. He believed God would help. But sometimes a man had to put his feet to prayers. Slowly, he turned in a three-sixty, surveying the Triple C as far as his eye could see. Someone had torched his land, but they wouldn't get that close again. Not with Whitney and the girls in the crosshairs.

He bundled the little family into the house and let Connie take over while he hustled into the dining room to meet Ace.

"Got your text, and we're all here like you asked." Like the other half dozen trusted cowboys in the room, Ace was on his feet. This wasn't a time to sit and chat. "What's going on?"

He told them everything he knew. Around the room the men bristled. One of them snarled like a mad dog. These were men he could depend on when the chips were down.

"I want to hire all of you to guard this ranch and Whitney and her girls. Starting now. Anyone not willing to carry a rifle for us is free to go. No hard feelings."

Not a man budged.

His throat filled with gratitude. He cleared it. Cowhands weren't comfortable with compliments, so he simply said, "Thanks. Gilbert will set up shifts. I'm headed to town to meet with the sheriff."

"I thought you just talked to Lawson," Ace said.

"Did. But whoever this hombre is threatened those I care about. I want to find him myself."

There was a general murmur of agreement. Cowboys didn't take kindly to anyone messing with their families.

"What about you, boss?" Beck rolled a weathered Stetson through his fingers. "The notes threatened you too. Maybe you should stay put, keep an eye on things around here, and let us and the sheriff handle the rest."

"I can take care of myself."

Ace shoved his hat down tight. "I'm going with you."

"Appreciate it. Let's ride."

FROM THE UPSTAIRS DORMER WINDOW, Whitney watched Nate's pickup truck speed away. She hadn't wanted him out her sight, but the stubborn man had gone anyway. If not for the twins, she'd have gone with him. This was her problem, too. Hers most of all. But her children came first. If staying behind protected them, she would let the sheriff deal with Ronnie Flood.

Tired and nervous, she still wasn't sure involving the sheriff was the right thing to do, but it was too late now.

She pressed her fingers against her forehead. The headache she'd been fighting all day was now full blown and throbbing. To make matters worse, the twins, feeling the tension in the air, were cranky as two badgers. When

Olivia whacked Sophia with a doll, Whitney scolded her. Then both girls wailed.

They needed a nap desperately. After not sleeping much for two nights, Whitney did too. Not that she expected to sleep. Not with Nate out there putting himself in danger. Not until Ronnie was found and this was over.

She pulled the twins onto the big bed and began to sing. At first, they flopped and whined, but soon they settled down. Olivia drifted off first, and Sophia wasn't far behind. Patting a bottom with each hand, Whitney closed her eyes and continued to hum softly.

She awakened to total darkness and a quiet house. Carefully, Whitney untangled her arms and legs from the twins. They remained asleep, identical behinds in the air. She pulled a corner of the comforter over them and eased off the bed to squeeze the button on her cell phone.

Midnight? They'd slept that long? She and the babies must have been exhausted from the tension. Surely, if there was news, someone would have awakened her.

Going to the window, she tugged the heavy drapes aside. From her room on the second floor, she searched for Nate's truck. She didn't see it. Had he parked in the back, or was he still out there somewhere? Searching, guarding?

Security lights chased back the heaviest darkness, illuminating the circle drive and the immediate lawn. Beyond lay pastureland and night as black as ink.

From the corner of her eye, she caught movement. A human shadow stretched across the lawn.

Her stomach tightened. Hair stood up on her neck.

A man with a rifle came into sight. Gilbert. Whitney exhaled. It was only Gilbert. Keeping watch.

For a while, she stood in the window and prayed, and

then, confident no harm would come to her babies with the Caldwell men on duty, she went back to bed.

THE NEXT THREE days passed in watchfulness. Nate, she discovered, had camped every night at her ranch, waiting for Ronnie to make his move. And every morning, against his protests, he and Ace escorted her home so she could feed her animals and pick up fresh clothes. They preferred she stayed inside the Triple C, behind locked doors. Yet, Nate put himself in harm's way day and night.

She felt like she was holding her breath, waiting for something to happen.

To keep her mind off the worry, Whitney and Connie made plans for the ranch rodeo, baked and froze a dozen pies, and cleaned the ranch house top to bottom. It was the least she could do to repay their hospitality.

Emily, too, had been convinced to bunk at the main house for a few days and spent evenings teaching Whitney how to design a basic website. All the while, men with rifles and cell phones patrolled the house and the perimeter of the Triple C. To no avail.

No sightings. No threats. No problems of any kind.

Early into the second week, everyone, especially Whitney, grew restless. Ronnie Flood seemed to have disappeared, and Arnold Leach claimed he was only trying to protect his client. Otherwise, he knew nothing useful.

Except for one patrolling guard, Ace decided to put the cowboys back to work. Nate was reluctant but he agreed. The Triple C couldn't run itself.

Slowly, Whitney relaxed. The worst must be over. If Ronnie knew the police were onto him, he would back off.

Anyway, that was the sheriff's theory. And no one could force her into forfeiting her ranch.

For two nights, she'd slept soundly, and today she awoke antsy to be busy, to get back home and begin preparations for the farm's very first Christmas event.

Olivia handed her a pair of Legos, which she snapped together before returning to the conversation with Nate. Sophia sat on the area rug nearby quietly turning the blocks this way and that, trying to discover for herself what her twin was too impatient to learn.

"Stay a few more days." Her rugged cowboy leaned in the doorway of the family room, weariness hanging on him like a wet blanket. He hadn't shaved in days. His eyes were bloodshot, and if not for a sharp rebuke from Connie, he'd have lived on nothing but portable coffee and sandwiches.

She pushed off the floor, went to him, and laid a hand on the side of his whiskery face. His tired smile barely reached his eyes.

That's when she made up her mind. Yes, being cherished and protected felt amazing, but not at the cost of Nate's well-being. Protection cut both directions. Like the sheriff, she was beginning to believe Ronnie had run like a scared rabbit the moment he'd learned she had back-up in the Caldwells.

"You've exhausted yourself, Nate, and for nothing. Go upstairs and get some rest. I'll go home." When he started to protest, she pressed a finger to his lips. "If I hear a twig snap or get a weird feeling, anything at all that hints at trouble, I'll call you."

He kissed her finger and pulled it down to his chest. "I don't think you should leave just yet."

"Even Sheriff Hawk thinks Ronnie's backed off and we're

probably safe now. Cowards often bolt when confronted."

"*Probably* isn't convincing enough."

She persisted. Granted, she was a little anxious about returning home with Ronnie's whereabouts still unknown, but fair was fair. "You need your life back."

He propped the ever-present rifle against the wall and glowered. "You and the twins *are* my life. As long as there is the slightest risk, I'll be watching."

"Exactly. You're watching. You have a guard on patrol day and night."

"If you go home, I'll have one at your house, too. Probably me."

"I'd like that—*after* you sleep eight hours."

He shook his head. "We need more time. Another day. Maybe two. Tomorrow I'll take you and the twins to OKC for the day. Get away from here, relax. What do you say? Stay with us a little longer. If you go home, I won't sleep. I'll worry."

Whitney leaned her forehead against his strong chest. To be loved like this was all she'd ever wanted. How could she say no?

"Okay. A few more days." She gave him a gentle push. "Now, upstairs, mister. Turn off that cell phone, lock the door, and sleep."

Taking the rifle, he did as she asked and trudged toward the staircase. She watched him, so full of love she wondered if a heart could explode with the emotion.

He paused halfway up the stairs to look back at her. Faking her meanest look, she pointed upward. He chuckled, gave her a wink, and disappeared into the upstairs.

With Nate resting and the twins playing happily, Whitney searched for something to do to stay busy. Connie had gone into town for groceries, and Emily was at work as usual. She and the twins had the big house all to themselves.

Feeling like a total freeloader, she schlepped into the kitchen. The window over the sink was smudged, so she grabbed the Windex and spritzed it.

"Looks like window cleaning is the project for the day." Anything to be useful to Connie and the other Caldwells.

The house was big, and with Nate asleep, she'd save the upstairs for later. She worked her way through the downstairs with frequent detours into the family room to play with the twins.

The room dubbed *the office* was at the back of the house and looked out over the barns and rows and rows of round hay bales. Standing on a chair, she was spraying the top window when something caught her eye.

She leaned closer, squinted. Was that Gilbert?

Blue liquid slithered down the pane and inhibited her view. She swiped at it with a paper towel.

"That's not Gilbert. Who—?" She stepped off the chair and set the Windex on the floor. Suddenly, flames erupted from a barn window. "Oh, no!"

She spun, stumbled over the Windex and slammed her ribcage against the chair. All the breath whooshed from her.

Fueled by adrenaline, she shook off the pain, jerked the cell phone from her back pocket, and shot Nate a text.

Then she ran for the barn.

"Gilbert! Ace!" Whitney looked wildly around for the ranch crew and saw no one. They had all gotten back to business today and could be anywhere on this eleven thousand acres. Even the patrol guard was absent.

That was wrong. Where was he?

With no time to spare, she raced to the water faucet and dragged the hose toward the barn. Smoldering smoke wafted in feathery tails from the window. No more flames. Yet.

Good. She'd gotten here in time.

She stuck the hose through the window and let it hang inside while she entered the barn in search of the source.

As she moved, she whipped the phone out. No response from Nate. She dialed his number. No answer.

Then she remembered. She'd insisted he shut off his phone.

She left a message and then pressed in Ace's number. It went to voice mail.

Frustrated, she shot texts to everyone she knew, including the sheriff.

Then she moved deeper into the barn. She owed the Caldwells. This was their winter hay. They'd already last a thousand acres of forage. She couldn't let this burn.

Whitney had learned enough to know wet hay could smolder for days and self-combust. Perhaps wet hay was the fire's source. She walked down the long center aisle, observing, seeking answers. The barn was quiet, dim, and smelled of smoke and chemicals.

As if a fist had reached into her chest and clamped down, her heart clutched.

Chemicals?

On alert, blood rushing through her head like Niagara Falls, she began backing toward the door.

Her back connected with something solid. Something human.

An elbow crooked around her neck. Strong arms locked hers against her sides.

A man whispered, "Keep quiet."

She struggled against him, trying to get a look at his face. He smelled of sweat and cologne...and chemicals. "Who are you? What do you want?"

She knew. Oh, she knew. Ronnie Flood had found her.

"You were warned. Why didn't you leave?" He tightened his forearm, narrowing her air supply. "Now, I'm forced to take matters into my own hands. And I do hate getting my hands dirty."

Whitney coughed. Her head started to spin. "I'll leave. I promise. Just let me go. The barn is on fire."

He laughed softly, fiendishly. Again the harsh whisper. "I warned you. Now you get to play the hero." He shoved her forward, his bigger, stronger body walking hers deeper into the barn. "Poor Whitney died trying to save her lover's barn. Which means you won't be able to inherit Sally's ranch after all. And no one will ever know I was here."

She stabbed her feet into the dirt floor. Her shoes skidded, slowing them down.

The elbow tightened on her throat. A rough shove propelled her forward. "Move."

Little gray dots danced before Whitney's eyes. She turned her head left then right, fighting the choke hold. The smoke thickened.

Her eyes streamed. Thought faded.

Help me. Jesus.

"Whitney!" Nate's voice ripped through her terror. "Are you in there?"

The man jerked her head back. "Keep quiet and I won't kill him."

She could barely breathe, much less speak. She wrestled against her captor, but he was too strong. With a powerful thrust, he shoved her toward the burning hay. She landed on the floor in a heap, gasping for air. Smoke billowed around her. She couldn't see. All she knew for sure was that her attacker was gone.

Staying low, she crawled forward, coughing, tears pouring from her eyes.

"Nate." The word sounded weak, raspy. "Nate. No. Get away."

A hulking shadow entered the room. She shrank closer to the floor, thrusting a hand out in search of a weapon. She braced herself to fight, to bite and scratch and claw. She would not let him choke her again, and she wouldn't let him get to Nate or her babies.

Finding no weapon, she grabbed a handful of dirt and crouched, ready to spring and catch him off guard.

Boots appeared before her streaming eyes. Roper boots. Nate's boots.

"Whitney. Oh, baby." Strong arms lifted her against his chest and carried her out of the barn.

When he'd set her on the ground and knelt beside her, she waved him away. "Stop the fire. Get Ronnie. It was him."

Nate's head whipped toward the driveway. "Ronnie Flood? He was here? But how?"

Whitney had no idea. She nodded, too breathless to say much. "The babies?"

"Connie's with them. Help is on the way." He kissed her tear-drenched face. "You sure you're okay?"

"Yes. The barn."

At her reassurance, he texted something and then raced toward the barn. After a few gulps of beautiful fresh air, Whitney struggled to her feet and went to help.

Nate was her cowboy. He wasn't going in there alone.

17

Hours later, the fire was out, and Whitney crashed on the Triple C couch like a dead woman. She *would* have been dead had it not been for Nate. He'd come for her. And right behind him had come the rest, along with the sheriff and the volunteer fire department. The crazy man hadn't shut off his phone after all.

She rolled her head toward her cowboy. He sat on the edge of the couch, watching as if he thought she'd disappear.

Connie, fretting like a mother hen, bustled into the family room, toting a tray of iced tea and cookies. She pressed a glass of tea into Whitney's hand. "Drink, *mija*. I will make a cold pack for your neck."

As the woman hurried away, Whitney levered up to one elbow and sipped. The cool tea eased the burning in her throat. Nate sipped at his own glass, his eyes on hers.

"You're some kind of woman."

She shook her head. "I couldn't let your barn burn down. Not after all you've done for me and the girls."

"But to rush back in there after what you'd been through." He clenched his hand so tight against the tumbler, Whitney thought it might break. "After what he put you through."

Whitney placed a hand on his knee. "I'm okay. We're all okay. The fire truck arrived in time, and we saved the barn and a winter's worth of hay."

He snorted. "I don't care about the hay or the barn. I can't lose you, Whitney."

"I know," she said, softly. For that brief instant when Ronnie had held her captive, she'd been so afraid she'd lured Nate into a trap. "I feel the same."

Smelling of smoke and love, he leaned in to kiss her. His cell vibrated. He made a face and straightened.

Ace, he mouthed to her as he pushed *answer*.

The brothers spoke for a few minutes and then Nate rang off. "Ace and the boys are on their way. They got him. It's over."

It took a beat for the statement to soak in. "Over? As in, Ronnie is in jail?"

"Ronnie has been arrested in Tulsa. And Arnold Leach is also in jail."

"My lawyer?" She dropped her feet to the floor and sat up. "I don't understand."

Gently, Nate took her tea glass and set it on the coffee table.

"He was the one who set the barn fire, but not the one in the pasture. Ronnie did that. He'd been doing all the dirty work for Leach. When word got out that he was the prime suspect, Flood got scared and ran."

"Mr. Leach admitted this?"

"Oh, no. But the boys caught him red-handed before he

ever got off the property. He claimed he was only on the Triple C today to speak to you about your inheritance. He wanted to be sure you and the girls were all right and to let you know he would do everything in his power to help you remain on your property."

Indignant, she stiffened. "He was the one who said I should leave!"

"He denied that, of course. Said you insisted he draw up that paper. He's a slick talker, that Leach. When he realized no one believed him, particularly since he had an empty accelerant can in his back seat, he asked for a lawyer and clammed up."

"So it will be my word against his." Whitney pressed a hand to her mouth. She was nobody. A high school dropout with a bad track record. Leach was a rich lawyer.

"No. My detective caught up with Ronnie Flood in Tulsa." Nate shot her a crooked grin. "Yeah, I hired a P.I. A good one, and Flood confessed everything. He was furious to be second in line to inherit Sally's property, so he and Leach hatched up a plan to drive you away."

"Why would Mr. Leach do such a thing?"

"Money. Ronnie stood to lose everything if you lasted out the year, but with Leach's help, he could still inherit. All he had to do was make life on the farm so miserable that you would run back to St. Louis."

"And I would default on the inheritance and give Ronnie the legal right to take over."

"That was the idea. Leach would take the other half for coming up with the plan, handling the paperwork, and all the other details that required a clever, scheming, legal mind. Without Leach, Ronnie was out in the cold for good."

"So my lawyer was the mastermind? To scare me away?"

Throat getting raw again, she reached for the tea and swigged, her mind whirling. "That still makes no sense. He's a rich man."

"Maybe once, but no more. The man's in gambling debt up to his eyebrows. Your ranch is prime real estate that he could sell at a nice profit and keep the debtors at bay. Plus, you own mineral rights, and according to Flood, Leach thinks there could be oil on your property. Another wad of cash for his coffers."

"But only if I didn't last the year."

"Exactly. Leach never expected a city girl with no experience to stick it out."

"He thought I would leave peacefully, and no one would be the wiser."

"That's about the size of it, but when he saw your grit, and your involvement with me, he moved on to threats."

"Which almost worked." She was so thankful she'd told Nate everything.

"But when you suspected something was amiss and refused to sign that paper, Leach got desperate. Then when Ronnie bailed, scared of discovery, the lawyer was on his own. He had to act."

"So he waited until all of you went back to work today to make his move."

"Apparently. Beck was on guard duty, but he was driving the fence next to your place, in case they tried something over there. Leach must have waited until he saw Beck pull out."

Whitney's head swam with the news. She was thrilled and shocked. And deeply relieved.

"So it's really over." They were safe, all of them, and the ranch was hers. "I can go home."

"Far as I'm concerned, you can stay here forever."

Forever. A word missing from her vocabulary.

"Oh, Nate. My Nate. My wonderful Nate." She sounded like the twins. *Nate, Nate, Nate.*

Whitney placed her hand on his rugged, handsome, whiskery cheek and lifted her face to kiss his jaw. Nate had other ideas and met her lips with his. Warm, supple, caring. Her cowboy. This man whose every action spoke of love.

"I love you, Whitney Brookes," he whispered against her ear. "Say you love me, too."

She tilted back, smiling, soft inside. "I love you, too, Nate Caldwell. You're the man I didn't know I was looking for, but I'm so glad you found me."

He chuckled softly. "Face down in the dirt on a country road."

What a beginning, and one she wouldn't trade for the world. Here, in Calypso with this man was where she belonged.

Against her chest, his big heart thudded wildly, beating for her.

Wrapped in contented joy and her man's strong arms, Whitney offered up a prayer of thanksgiving.

She had called in her distress, broken, lost, alone and scared.

And God had answered with a cowboy.

EPILOGUE

The sky threatened rain that April Saturday, but a few cranky clouds didn't stop the Easter bunny or the dozens of excited, giggling children who came to Twin Hope Miniature Farm's very first Easter Egg-stravaganza.

"Your city girl has become quite an entrepreneur."

Nate grinned at Ace's description. "And to think, at one time I thought a miniature animal farm was a useless hobby."

"Amazing, isn't it?" Ace removed his hat and scratched at his ear. "If the crowds that hit this place on weekends are any indication, Whitney's onto a good thing. The petting zoo is popular rain or shine. And your idea of selling cups of feed for the chickens and bottles of milk for the baby goats wasn't half bad."

Nate snorted at his brother. "From you, that's high praise."

"Yeah, well, don't let it go to your head. That lady of yours is the real brains of the outfit."

"No argument from me." Nate looked around for the lady in question, his gaze lingering on the cheerful, happy scene. Whitney had worked her tail off—and his too, he thought in amusement—to turn her inheritance into a family-friendly venue.

Kids of all ages toted baskets of colorful plastic eggs filled with prizes and roamed in and out of the petting barn. Youth from the church manned the egg hunts, ticket booth, and concessions. Pastel Easter decorations lined the entry, and a big sign next to a huge cardboard bunny declared "Hoppy Easter!"

It was cute. It was fun. It was spring-like, but Nate's favorite spot was a small flower garden near the house dedicated to the true meaning of Easter. White lilies surrounded three wooden crosses with the center cross draped in red cloth. A yard stake proclaimed, "He is risen." On the double row of chairs next to the garden, two young families sat in quiet contemplation.

At sundown, something else was going to happen there, and he couldn't wait.

"Want something to drink?" Ace's voice broke through his thoughts. "The concession is calling my name."

"Nah, you go on." Nate was glad to see his brother headed to the soda pop instead of his former beverage of choice. "My woman's smiling my way. Think I'll go over and marry her right now."

"Patience, son. Patience." With a laugh, Ace thumped his back and moved away. Nate did the same.

He'd been patient long enough. Today was the day.

Whitney met him halfway, long hair floating behind and a smile as wide as the horizon.

His heart music began to sing. The pleasure lifted him, made him feel weightless.

"Hey, gorgeous. Where are the twins?"

Before answering, she leaned in for her kiss. Nate didn't mind one bit.

"Over there with Emily. She and Connie are going to get them dressed for me pretty soon." She pointed toward the open area where the egg hunts had occurred. The girls, in denim overalls and red tennis shoes, sat on the ground with their soon-to-be aunt and dug through their filled baskets. "They adore her."

"She feels the same." He removed his hat, swiped imaginary sweat, and put it back on. "My sister needs kids of her own."

"I agree." Whitney looped her arm with his and pressed into his side, face upturned. "But she told me she'll never marry again."

"Told me the same. After Dennis died, she closed off. I guess losing two loves was too many."

"Two?" Whitney tilted her head to one side. "She lost someone else?"

"Not lost as in death. Not like Dennis. But when she was in high school, there was this cowboy. Scott Donley's brother, Levi. Good guy. Still don't know what happened. They were crazy in love. We all knew they'd marry as soon as they graduated."

"But they didn't."

"No. She's never told us what happened, but Levi left Calypso and never came back. Emily was shattered, drew inside herself. Dad was real worried. We all were. When she met Dennis, we thought she'd finally found happiness."

"And then he died. Oh, Nate, that's so tragic."

"The Caldwell siblings haven't been too lucky in love. Until now." He touched her cheek. "Sure you want to marry this stodgy old cowpoke today?"

"I want to marry the best man I've ever known, the handsomest, hardest working, kindest cowboy God ever made."

"That leaves me out."

She laughed and whacked his arm. "Don't try to get out of this, buster."

"Not a chance. I just wish all these people would hurry up and go home."

"It's time, honey."

Three hours later, the customers were gone and the guests were arriving. Whitney peeked out the bedroom window at the cars and pickups parked in her driveway. Friends from church and the Caldwells. Not a big group but all the right people to celebrate a day she had only dreamed of. Certainly a day she'd never expected to have in Calypso, Oklahoma.

"Whitney. Honey, come on. Time to get dressed."

Whitney moved away from the window to aim a teary smile at her mother. "I still can't believe you're here. After you said Dad had a conference this weekend—"

When she'd seen her parents coming across the decorated lawn, she'd burst into tears.

"We're so pleased to see how your life has changed. This is icing on the cake. Conferences come and go. This is family." Mom held out the wedding gown. "Now put this on and get out there in that beautiful garden and marry that fine man."

Family. At last. Sniffling, heart full, Whitney slipped her arms into the dress and let the material float to the floor in a soft swirl.

As she stepped into her shoes, Mom added a garland of tiny white flowers to her hair.

Whitney went to the long mirror. "Is that me?"

"You look radiant, honey. Like a woman should on her wedding day."

She felt like a fairy, like a princess. Like a woman in love.

A knock sounded on the door. "About ready in there? The preacher and the groom are getting antsy."

"Don't let him run away," she called.

The voice behind the door, Ace's, she thought, laughed. "Fat chance. You're stuck with him. We have a no-returns policy at the Triple C."

With one last glance in the mirror, she stepped onto the porch, placed her hand in the crook of her father's elbow, and started the short trek toward the garden. Pastel lights draped the setting. Connie's carefully planted flowers bloomed in profusion as if they'd known today was special.

She and Nate had chosen this day on purpose, the day before Easter, before Resurrection Day. A time of new beginnings.

The twins, wearing fluffy white dresses with pastel sashes, walked before her, spreading rose petals on the green grass. When they spotted their hero, they forgot the roses and raced ahead. Nate stood in front of the gathering between his brother and the pastor, handsome in dark jeans, white shirt, black boots, and jacket. Simple. And perfect.

"Nate, my Nate," Olivia cried as she threw her arms around his legs in high drama. The small gathering tittered.

Nate dropped a hand to Olivia's head and murmured something, but his eyes remained on Whitney.

Her stomach fluttered. Pleasure rose in her chest as she walked down the grassy aisle between the rows of folding chairs to her true love.

"Mommy's pitty," Sophia said, patting the skirt of Whitney's wedding gown.

"She's beautiful." Nate reached out a hand.

Whitney grasped the work roughened palm of her cowboy and moved into place beside him. At his side. Where she always wanted to be.

Out in the barn a donkey brayed, Clive whinnied, and Mick Jagger crowed. The billy goat rammed his head into the gate, and at the noise, two nannies tumbled to the ground in a faint.

Too full of joy to hold it all in, Whitney and her cowboy looked at each other and laughed.

And the wedding began.

ABOUT THE AUTHOR

Winner of the RITA Award for excellence in inspirational fiction, Linda Goodnight has also won the Booksellers' Best, ACFW Book of the Year, and a Reviewers' Choice Award from Romantic Times Magazine. Linda is a New York Times bestselling author.

Linda has appeared on the Christian bestseller list and her romance novels have been translated into more than a dozen languages. Active in orphan ministry, this former nurse and teacher enjoys writing fiction that carries a message of hope and light in a sometimes dark world.

She and husband Gene live in Oklahoma with their daughters.

www.lindagoodnight.com

ALSO BY LINDA GOODNIGHT

Triple C Cowboys

Twins for the Cowboy

A Baby for the Cowboy

A Bride for the Cowboy

Honey Ridge

The Memory House

The Rain Sparrow

The Innkeeper's Sister

The Buchanons

Cowboy Under the Mistletoe

The Christmas Family

Lone Star Dad

Lone Star Bachelor

Whisper Falls

Rancher's Refuge

Baby in His Arms

Sugarplum Homecoming

The Lawman's Honor

Redemption River

Finding Her Way Home

The Wedding Garden

A Place to Belong

The Christmas Child

The Last Bridge Home

The Brothers' Bond

A Season for Grace

A Touch of Grace

The Heart of Grace

52796651R00151

Made in the USA
Middletown, DE
21 November 2017